Praise for Witch Mountain

"Action, mood, and characterization never falter in this superior science fiction novel."

—Library Journal

"Fantasy, science fiction, mystery, adventure—the story is all of these, with enough suspense and thrills to keep young readers glued to its pages from first to last."

—Book World

"A tantalizing and perceptive...book for boys and girls."

—America

"Fascinating science fiction."

*—Elementary School Library Collection,
Brodart Foundation*

ESCAPE
TO
WITCH
MOUNTAIN

ALEXANDER KEY

SOURCEBOOKS
Jabberwocky
AN IMPRINT OF SOURCEBOOKS

Published by Jabberwocky, an imprint of Sourcebooks, Inc.
P.O. Box 4410, Naperville, Illinois 60567-4410
(630) 961-3900
Fax: (630) 961-2168
www.jabberwockykids.com

Library of Congress Cataloging-in-Publication Data is on file with the publisher.

Printed and bound in the United States of America
VP 10 9 8 7 6 5 4 3 2 1

To All Orphans, Of All Worlds

CONTENTS

STAR BOX

Tony, carrying their bags, followed his sister, Tia, and the welfare worker down the tenement steps to the sidewalk. While the welfare worker unlocked her car, Tony looked unhappily around at the ugly world of South Water Street, knowing he was seeing it for the last time. He and Tia had never loved it—it wasn't the world they belonged to—but at least it had been home.

For a moment, as he stood there, he wondered again about the world they had come from, and if they would ever find it. In what direction it lay, or how one got there, he hadn't the slightest idea.

"Maybe," Tia had once said, "all we have to do is climb a certain stairway, or go around a strange corner—and there it'll be."

"Just like that," he'd said, laughing.

"Why not?" she'd insisted. "We know the *kind* of place it is. It's full of magic and music—for that's the *only* kind of place we could have come from. So why wouldn't we have to find it sort of magically?"

Maybe it didn't exactly make sense, the way Tia had put it, but he was sure of one thing. Considering how unlike other people they were, it was the only kind of world they could have come from—so it *must* be somewhere.

The welfare worker said irritably, "We haven't got all day. Put your things in the car."

"Where—where are we going?" Tony asked uneasily.

"To Hackett House, of course."

*   *   *

On the other side of the city, Tony stared in dismay at the gaunt old brick building, with its high iron fence surrounding the bare play yard. The place seemed almost like a jail. Then he remembered that Hackett House was more of a detention home than an orphanage, for orphans in good standing were never sent here.

Inside, Miss Trask, the welfare worker, presented them to Mrs. Grindley, the matron, who had once been a policewoman. From the expressionless way Mrs. Grindley looked them over—as if she were viewing a pair of strange and doubtful fish that had been dredged up from the harbor depths—Tony knew that the days ahead were not going to be overflowing with sweetness and light. At that moment he was extremely conscious of the differences that set Tia and himself apart from others: their pale hair and olive skins, their slenderness, and their dark-blue eyes that were almost black.

Mrs. Grindley gave a baffled shake of her head. "I can't place these two, Miss Trask. Where did they come from?"

"That South Water Street area near the docks," replied the welfare worker a little wearily. "They lived there with an old woman. No known relatives. Exact ages unknown. Nationality doubtful. My office hasn't had time to check their school records, but the police say the boy has a bad reputation for fighting. The girl has been accused of theft—"

"The police were wrong!" Tony interrupted. "Tia went into that building to take a kitten out of a trap. She's a softie for cats. She never—"

"Shut up," the matron told him in her flat voice. "And don't ever let me catch you fighting here, or you'll learn what trouble is. Go on, Miss Trask."

"Well, for the past ten years, they've been living with this old woman they called their grandmother—a Mrs. Nellie Malone. She was struck by a taxi yesterday and died. The children have been using her name, but we've discovered they are just unknown orphans Mrs. Malone took in."

"I see." Mrs. Grindley glanced at Tia, whose thin elfin face was pinched with misery, then at Tony, who stood half a head taller. "Have you any idea what your real name is, or where you came from?"

The questions had become the most important ones in Tony's life, but at the moment he could only look at her bleakly and give a mumbled "No, ma'am." The shock of losing Granny Malone was still with him. She was the only person who cared for Tia and himself, and the hurt went deep.

"Very well," Mrs. Grindley said. "Now, I want it understood that we have strict rules here—much stricter than in most juvenile homes. You will find them posted in the main hall. Read them carefully. If you disobey them, or cause any trouble, you will be punished. You might even be sent to a correctional institution. Is that clear?"

"Yes, ma'am," said Tony, and Tia nodded.

Mrs. Grindley frowned at Tia. "Answer when you're spoken to."

Tony's mouth tightened. "Tia can't talk, ma'am."

Miss Trask raised her eyebrows. "I'm surprised to hear that. The investigating officer didn't mention it. Weren't you two whispering together on the way over here?"

"It was my voice you heard, not Tia's," Tony said. "They'll tell you about her when you check at our school." He thought it wiser not to mention that Tia *could* talk, at least to him, though it wasn't the sort of speech that anyone else could hear. The world, he had learned, didn't like people who were different, and the less others knew about the two of them, the better. Even Granny Malone hadn't known very much.

"We'll let the doctor worry about her," said Mrs. Grindley. Shrugging, she looked at the welfare woman. "Did you search them, Miss Trask?"

"I looked only at the things that were packed. They've nothing they're not allowed to have, unless it's on their persons."

"I'll see to that. Come here, boy."

Tony stood in front of her. The matron's big hands went swiftly through his clothing. She missed nothing, not even the three ten-dollar bills he had taken from his billfold and pinned in the waistband of his trousers for greater safety. She seemed disappointed that the search produced nothing more deadly than a harmonica, a tiny doll carved from a finger-sized bit of wood, and a small pocketknife.

"Knives," she said, not unkindly, "are strictly forbidden here." She prodded the doll, which had jointed legs and feet. "What are you doing with this thing?"

"I—I made it. Tia has one like it."

She grunted and thrust everything back at him except the knife and the three ten-dollar bills. "You may keep the small change, but I'd better lock up the tens, or they'll be stolen from you. Where did you get so much money?"

"I worked for it."

"Tell me a better one. School's hardly out for the summer. You haven't had time to earn anything."

"I've been doing odd jobs after school for several years." He could have told her it was to help pay for his clothes and Tia's, for Granny's pension had been stretched to the limit. "Would you like the names and telephone numbers of the people I worked for?"

"On South Water Street? Don't bother." Mrs. Grindley's world-weary eyes went to Tia, and fastened on the box dangling by its strap from Tia's small wrist. It was a curious box with rounded corners, made of a dark leather that had been beautifully tooled. On either side, done in gold leaf, was a striking design in the form of a double star, with each star having eight points. Mrs. Grindley pulled the box from Tia's wrist, pawed through its contents, then closed it and sat frowning at it.

"Miss Trask, did you ever see anything like this?"

The welfare worker shook her head. "The thing's a work of art. I've been wondering how this girl acquired it."

"I can guess," the matron said dryly.

Tia's pointed chin trembled. Tony fought down his temper. You couldn't argue with authority, especially when it had already made up its mind about you. "The star box is rightfully Tia's," he managed to say quietly. "She's had it all her life. Please give it back. She needs it to carry her notebook and pencils in—without them she can't write answers to people."

The matron shrugged and tossed the box to Tia. "If you want to keep it here, you'd better put it in your locker at night."

The star box, which had always attracted some attention, was to take them away from Hackett House in time. But in the beginning it was almost their undoing.

The day after their arrival it was snatched from Tia as she was leaving the dining room, and done so cleverly that no one saw it happen. Only Tony was able to hear her cry, and he raced into the main hall in time to glimpse the snatcher, a small frightened youth half his size, vanishing up the stairway that led to the boys' dormitory.

When he reached the dormitory the star box had changed hands, and Tony found himself facing the dormitory leader, a big fellow the others called Truck.

It was immediately evident that the box had been taken at Truck's order. No matter what happened, Truck would have to be deposed.

Tony felt a cold prickling as he realized the corner he was in. Last night up here, just before lights out, Truck had confronted him, saying, "All new guys gotta divvy up their dough. That's my rule. And no ratting to old Grindstone; anybody rats, I cut my initials on 'em with this." Truck had produced a thin, sharpened piece of steel—a homemade dagger known as a shiv—and thrust the point of it against Tony's chest.

Last night, with the point of the shiv bringing a spot of blood to his shirt, and Mrs. Grindley's warning against fighting still ringing in his ears, he had submitted to the indignity of being robbed. But today it was different. The star box was the only clue he and Tia had to the strange world of their past. To lose it was unthinkable. Nor could he expect any help from Mrs. Grindley or her staff—by the time he could get help, he knew the box would be gone and every boy here would deny having seen it.

Truck swung the box tauntingly in his face. "Looking for something, Pretty Boy?"

With a movement too swift for any of the watching eyes to follow, Tony caught up the box and tossed it under a cot for safety. Then, evading a vicious kick and a jab, he went grimly to work, using every trick he knew.

Tony's tricks included most of the old ones, plus a few odd ones of his own, for he had been forced into many fights before the incredulous gangs of his neighborhood had learned to avoid him. But he was not yet adept at taking a sharp weapon away from a suddenly frenzied opponent the size of Truck. A pillow he snatched up for protection was quickly slashed, and he received two bad cuts before he was able to send the shiv flying mysteriously across the room. After that it was easy. The gaping group of boys in the dormitory saw Truck whirled about and slammed into the wall with a sound that was heard all over the building. Truck was still lying there, dazed, when Mrs. Grindley charged into the room.

Tony was spattered with blood and feathers. He felt a little sick. Fighting was distasteful enough, but it was all the more hateful because it drew attention to himself. Now he chilled as he saw the implacable face of the matron.

He expected to be punished. That alone did not worry him—but suppose he was separated from Tia and sent away to reform school? How could poor Tia ever manage alone? It was a frightening thought.

A doctor stitched up his arm. Later, Mrs. Grindley put him on the mat. She had already disposed of Truck by turning him over to the police.

It did no good for Tony to protest that he hadn't started the fight. Why, if the star box had been taken, hadn't he asked for help instead of trying to settle matters himself? To his obvious answer, Mrs. Grindley shook her head. "That's no excuse. I warned you about fighting. Now you'll have to take the consequences."

She paused a moment and looked at him strangely. "Tony, I would have said it was physically impossible for anyone like you to do what you did to Truck. How did you manage it?"

It was the sort of question that was always asked, and he dreaded it. "I—I'm just quicker than most people, I suppose." He swallowed. "Are you going to send me away?"

"Not this time. But all your privileges are canceled, and you will be restricted to the dormitory for the next two weeks."

He managed to look glum, but he felt like shouting.

During his stay in the dormitory, the other boys gladly took turns bringing up his meals. With their help, Tia smuggled books to him from the small library she had discovered in the front of the building. No one suspected that he talked with Tia daily.

He accomplished it by standing at a rear window in the boys' wing, and peering out over the kitchen roof until Tia appeared in the far corner of the playground. It was the only part of the playground he could see, and ordinarily, with all the noises of the city about them, it would have taken much shouting to be heard from such a distance. But between Tia and himself shouting was unnecessary, and their lips barely moved. It was, he had once reasoned out, a sort of ultrasonic speech that could be heard by no one who was not blessed with the most acute sense of hearing. Only, he had often wondered, why couldn't Tia speak normally?

Tia began smuggling books to him during his first week upstairs. The library, he learned later, was a musty little room crammed with old cast-off volumes that almost no one ever bothered to read. Even so, Mrs. Grindley, who seemed to have a hatred of books, insisted upon keeping the place locked most of the time. Tia, however, was able to enter it. To her, it was a shining gold mine—as all libraries were.

"It's got seven sets of encyclopedias!" she called to him from the corner of the play yard. "*Seven!* Isn't that perfectly wonderful?"

Tony agreed that it was wonderful, and groaned when she said she was sending him a book on botany, and another on woodcraft.

Tia said, "I want you to read all about genus Toxicodendron—that's poison ivy."

"What for?" he asked curiously. Woodcraft was great, even though he had never been in the woods; but botany was for the birds.

"Because there's all kinds of Toxicodendron up at Heron Lake—and that's where everybody's going soon. On vacation. The city is sending us to Heron Lake Camp for a *whole week!* Don't say anything about it because we aren't supposed to know it yet."

Tony didn't ask how she'd heard. Often, Tia seemed to know things without being told. Part of it, of course, was her memory. Tia never forgot anything.

Suddenly excited at the prospect of being able to leave the city, if only for a week, Tony closed his eyes and tried to visualize Heron Lake Camp. It wasn't always possible to visualize places he had never seen, but sometimes he could manage it. He heard Tia, who was just as excited, call wistfully, "Can you *see* it, Tony?"

"I think so."

"What's it like?"

The picture that came into focus behind his closed eyes, as real as a movie film, was a little disappointing. Heron Lake—if that was what he saw—was hardly more than a man-made pond; it was surrounded by a few scrawny pines, with some barrackslike buildings on one side. It was just the sort of place, he thought, that poor city kids were always being sent to in droves. He could see them swarming around it now, and crowding a muddy strip of beach till there was hardly standing room.

"Oh, it's O.K.," he told her. "Anyway, I'd sure rather be there than here, and I'll take the poison ivy."

"So will I. Tony, something's going to happen at Heron Lake."

"What?"

"I don't know. But it's going to happen. I feel it."

*   *   *

A chartered bus took them away from the hot city one July morning, and dropped them at slightly cooler Heron Lake Camp a few hours later. The place looked exactly as he had seen it in his mind except for one important detail, which had been hidden by the barrackslike buildings. There were mountains on the horizon. Mountains, misty blue and mysterious in the distance.

Tony stared at them, entranced. He had often visualized mountains, but these were the first real ones he had ever seen. He felt Tia clutch his arm, and knew the sight affected her the same way. There was a curious appeal in mountains. Somehow, he was certain, they were going to be very important in their lives.

It was a feeling that did not leave him during their entire week at Heron Lake. But it was not until their final day—their final minute, in fact—that anything unusual happened.

There was much confusion that morning. The incoming buses, jammed with new children, were arriving before the outgoing buses were ready to leave. While they waited in line to get aboard, a car stopped near them and two gray-robed nuns got out. The smaller one, who seemed much older than the other, glanced at Tia and saw the star box dangling from her wrist.

"What an unusual box," the nun exclaimed softly, as she came over and stooped beside Tia. "My dear child, where did you get it?"

"Tia's always had it," said Tony. "We don't know where it came from. I—I wish we did."

The nun touched the gold design with a delicate finger. She was a frail little person, with deeply sunken eyes. "A double star!" she whispered. "And done in gold leaf. That's very uncommon. I teach design, and I've seen this particular one used only once before in my life. It was on a letter."

"A letter?" Tony repeated wonderingly. "Would—would you mind telling us about it?"

"It was several years ago," the little nun said. "A man wrote to me, asking for information about certain unusual aptitudes in my pupils. Apparently it was for some research he was doing. Anyway, I remember his letter had a double star at the top of it. It was exactly like this one, with the same number of points. And it was even printed in gold."

Tony was speechless for a moment. The confusion and the rumbling bus being loaded beside him were forgotten. That curious, unknown world seemed just around the comer.

Suddenly he begged, "Please, can you give us the man's name? We don't know who our people are, and he may be a relation."

The nun pressed her thin hand to her forehead. "It was something like Caroway, or Garroway. No, Hideaway seems closer—though that couldn't be it. Anyway, I do recall that he lived in the mountains, but much farther south. Somewhere down in the Blue Ridge."

Tony gasped. "The mountains—the Blue Ridge? You're sure?"

"Yes, because he mentioned them. He said—"

They were interrupted by the bus driver, who shouted, "Hey, you kids! Get aboard—or aren't you going to Hackett House?"

"Wait!" Tony pleaded. "Just a moment—please!"

"I ain't got all day," the driver grumbled.

The nun said hastily, "The letter may be on file at the school. When I get back tonight I'll look it up. If you'll give me your names…"

Tia was already swiftly scribbling their names and address on a piece of notepaper. The nun took it and folded it away, saying, "I'm Sister Amelia, of St. Agnes School. If I can find the letter, I'll—"

Her voice was drowned by the roar of another bus approaching. They were forced to separate as two other nuns came over and took Sister Amelia by the arms. Tony had no chance to talk to her again. Reluctantly he followed Tia aboard.

He was in a daze of excitement and uncertainty all the way back to the city.

OUT OF YESTERDAY

At Hackett House that night, Tony lay awake long after the other boys had gone to sleep. Somewhere in the mountains was a man who was almost certainly a member of the same family as Tia and himself. It had to be that way. Why else the double star? You wouldn't use such an uncommon design on a letter—and print it so exactly—without reason.

It was galling not to know that person's name, or where he lived. Everything depended on Sister Amelia. So much depended on her, in fact, that it suddenly worried him to realize he didn't know her address. She'd merely said St. Agnes School, as if she thought he knew where it was—but St. Agnes School might be in any of a dozen towns within a few hours' drive of Heron Lake.

The next day he borrowed the telephone directories and searched through them carefully. St. Agnes School was not listed in the city, or in any of the suburbs.

He told himself it didn't really matter, for surely they'd hear from Sister Amelia within a day or two.

But three long days passed and dragged into four; then four became five, and five turned into six. Finally a new week had begun, and still there was no word from the little nun.

Tony despaired. What could have happened? Had Sister Amelia lost the paper Tia had given her? Or, worse, had she been unable to find the all-important letter?

"No," said Tia to the last question. "She'd write if she could, no matter what. I'm *sure* of that, Tony. She knows how important it is. I—I'm awfully afraid about her. She's old, and I know she wasn't at all well when we saw her..."

They had finished their assigned tasks for the afternoon, and had met in the tiny library. It was the only spot where they could talk without interruption. The place was stifling. Tony unlocked the front window and opened it for ventilation. He peered glumly out at the ceaseless traffic and the old rooming houses across the street.

What were they going to do?

Absently he took the tiny wooden doll from his pocket, placed it on the windowsill, and pointed his finger at it. Feeling as he did, his curious ability to make things move was at a low ebb. The doll lay crumpled and motionless until he found his harmonica and blew a few soft notes. Gradually, life seemed to enter it. It stirred, rose slowly, and finally began to dance as he played. The music was Tony's own, the softest whisper of a melody that came from somewhere deep within him. Tia listened, entranced, then opened the star box. Now the other doll joined the first upon the windowsill.

The drab world around them was forgotten. Here for a moment there was magic. Magic in the music, in the dancing dolls, and in the thought that somewhere, surely, there was a magical place where they would find other people like themselves.

Could it really be in the mountains? And why there?...

Tony stopped playing, and bleak reality returned. Reluctantly, the dolls and the harmonica were put away.

Tia said, "If you try *hard*, maybe you can *see* the man who wrote Sister Amelia. Then, if you could see where he *lives*..."

"I've been trying," he grumbled. "But when you don't know what to look for...Tia, we've got to be practical. The first thing is to locate St. Agnes School."

"It must be listed somewhere. If we could get the right directory—"

"Oh, any priest ought to know where it is. What's the name of that one we met once? He runs that place down where South Water Street nears the bridge."

"Father O'Day," Tia said instantly. "At St. Paul's Mission."

"Well, I've heard he's a pretty good Joe. I'm sure he'd help us. I'd like to go and see him—if Mrs. Grindley will let me—and tell him all about things." Tony paused and searched through his jeans. He scowled at the four pennies he found, and added, "I ought to phone him first, but I'll need six more cents. Have you any money?"

Tia looked startled. "Why—why yes. I've *lots* of money. I meant to tell you, but I was so *worried* about Sister Amelia…" She reached deep into the star box and handed him a folder of paper. "I don't know how much is there," she added.

It was just like her, he thought, to ignore any money she'd found. She'd always said that there must be something very bad about money, because those who needed it most never had it, and so many who had it would do such awful things to get more of it.

The folder, he saw, was part of an old road map, badly worn. He opened it slowly, and stared. Inside were nine twenty-dollar bills, and two fives.

"Tia!" he whispered, hardly believing his eyes. "Where'd you get all this?"

"From the bottom of the star box. I mean, from *between* the bottoms. It's been there all the time."

"But, Tia—"

"The star box has *two* bottoms, see?" She opened it and showed him the removable piece that fitted tightly inside. It had been loose for some time, she explained. Last night she took it out to fix it, and found the folder of money.

"I don't get it," he muttered. "Why would money be hidden in your box? You ought to be able to remember something about it. Can't you?"

"Tony, all I know is that I had the box when we came to live with Granny Malone. I've tried and tried, but that's as far back as my memory goes."

He shook his head. Tia's memory was the queerest thing he'd ever heard of. It was practically perfect up to a point, then it stopped cold. Of course, they were pretty young when they first came to live with Granny, and it was surprising that Tia could recall anything at all of that time. He himself could remember nothing.

"I'm going to keep one of the fives," he said. "Better hide the rest where you found it."

He was carefully tucking the bill into a secret compartment of his wallet when something dark appeared on the windowsill and leaped down at Tia's feet. It was a small black cat. Tia seemed to be acquainted with it, for she scooped it up happily and hugged it.

"It's Winkie," she said. "He's my cat."

"*Your* cat?"

"Of course he's my cat, aren't you, Winkie?" Winkie gave a meow, and she said, "He's very, very special, and we understand each other perfectly. He slips into the girls' dorm every night and sleeps on my cot."

"You'd better not let Mrs. Grindley find out about it. She hates cats."

The words were hardly spoken when his ears detected, above the countless other sounds in the building and the street outside, the familiar thud of Mrs. Grindley's low-heeled shoes approaching in the hall. Tia, whose hearing was equally acute, gave a little gasp and said, "Run, Winkie! Run!"

Winkie, reluctant to leave, had scampered only as far as the corner of the windowsill when the door was thrust open and Mrs. Grindley entered.

The matron saw the black cat on the instant. "Scat!" she cried, and seized the first book in reach and hurled it. It curved curiously and struck the wall, and Winkie vanished outside.

"Who let that animal in here?" Mrs. Grindley asked.

"It just came in," Tony replied.

"And who opened the window?"

"I did, ma'am. It's hot in here."

"I'm not concerned with the heat. Close that window this instant, and lock it."

Tony did as he was told.

"Now, young man," she began, "suppose you tell me what you two are up to, and how you managed to get in."

"B-but it's a library, isn't it?" Tony said defensively. "We always come in here to get books to read."

"Through a locked door?" The matron's voice was icy.

"It wasn't locked when I came here," Tony insisted.

"Don't lie to me. I locked the door last night, and I haven't unlocked it since. You must be using a skeleton key to get in. Where is it?"

"We don't have one, ma'am. Honest!"

"I know better." She began to search them.

The search was thorough, and there were tense moments when Tony held his breath, fearful that the matron would discover the five dollars hidden in his billfold, or worse, the bulk of the money in the star box. The discovery would have been disastrous, for he knew she would never accept the truth. As for entering the library, he hadn't lied, for the door *had* been open. Only, Tia had opened it before he arrived. That was another thing he knew better than to try to explain to anyone.

If it was *right* to open a door, Tia could always manage it. All she had to do was turn the knob, and any lock would yield. But she'd learned very early that if it was *wrong* to open it, then the door wouldn't budge. Of course, the police hadn't agreed that it was right, that time they'd caught Tia way in the back of a grocery where she'd gone to take the kitten out of a trap. In the first place, they hadn't believed it possible for anyone to hear a kitten crying that far away, through a closed door. On top of it, the store had already been robbed a couple times. They'd made it rough for Tia, but it hadn't changed how she felt. She'd do anything for animals.

Mrs. Grindley, intent upon her search for a key, overlooked the money. Failing to find any object even resembling a key, she stepped back and surveyed them. Tony could sense her baffled anger.

"I don't know what it is," she said, "but there's something about you two I don't understand. I'll be glad when I can get rid of you. In the meantime, I'm locking this place up and I never want to catch either of you in here again. Now get out."

There were tears in Tia's eyes as Tony followed her out to the playground. The library, he knew, was the only thing that made Hackett House bearable for her. As for himself, it didn't matter too much. The world was a tough place. You had to see it for what it was, and keep fighting it, or it would beat you down.

At the moment, his main worry was how he was going to get in touch with Father O'Day. The only telephone in Hackett House was in Mrs. Grindley's office, and inmates were not allowed to use it except in an emergency. The nearest public telephone was in a pharmacy two blocks away. He had hoped to get permission to go there, but the matron would never give him permission now. He would have to sneak out tonight.

He sat down unhappily in the shade of the building and took out his harmonica. For a while, sure there was no one around to notice him, he passed the time by making pebbles bounce across the playground like rubber balls. Then he saw that Tia was watching a taxi that had stopped by the sidewalk on the other side of the fence. All Tia's attention was on the passenger that had stepped out and was now paying the driver. She was staring at the man as if she were seeing a ghost.

"What's the matter?" he asked.

Tia did not answer. She moved closer to the fence, one hand pressed to her mouth. Her eyes were frightened.

Tony hurried over beside her and peered through the fence. The taxi was pulling away, and the man had turned and was lighting a cigarette while he looked up at the Hackett House entrance. He was slender and dark, and a little too old for Tony to make much of a guess at his age. Down on South Water Street they would have called him a sharp dresser, for he was wearing an expensive brown silk suit, with a pale brown shirt and matching tie. Tony ruled out Italian, and decided he was either a Greek or an Armenian.

"Tia!" he whispered. "What's the matter?"

"I—I know him, Tony."

He shook his head. "He's a stranger. I never saw him before."

"Yes, you have. You just don't remember him."

"Then who is he?"

She closed her eyes and said in her tiny voice, "He—*he's the man who left us with Granny Malone.*"

Tony's mouth fell open with shock. He turned his head, staring, but the man had already climbed the steps and disappeared into the Hackett House vestibule.

He swallowed, and managed to say, "How can you be sure? You never said anything about him before."

"I didn't remember him till I saw his face. Then it came back. I—I almost know his name. If I don't try too hard…"

"Where did he bring us from?"

"I—I don't know, Tony. It seems as if I should know, but I just can't remember anything else."

Tony thrust his hands deep into his jeans and worriedly scuffed the gravel with the toe of one shoe. "I don't get it, Tia. What's he doing here?"

Tia looked frightened. "I don't know. I—I'm afraid he's found out we're here, and has come to get us."

"After all these years? That doesn't make sense. But what if he *has* come for us? I'd rather go with him any time than stay here—I mean, if we *had* to stay here."

"No!" she said fiercely. "No! Never! It would be better to run away and go hungry. *Much* better. I—I'd rather be dead than go with him."

Tony didn't argue with her. Tia could feel things he couldn't, and he'd learned it always paid to follow her instincts. "I don't suppose," he muttered, "that he could be the same guy who wrote to Sister Amelia. I hope not."

"Oh, no! The names are different. The man in the mountains had a name like Garroway or Hideaway. But this man…it's Der—Der—" She paused, then said, "It's Deranian! His first name is Lucas."

Lucas Deranian. It sounded Armenian, Tony thought. And what was Lucas Deranian up to?

They waited uneasily. Minutes passed. After a long while a boy ran out into the playground and told them they were wanted in the office.

Mrs. Grindley was seated behind her desk when they entered. She looked at them stolidly, saying nothing, but at her nod the man in the brown suit rose from his chair, tucking away a silk handkerchief with which he had been lightly mopping his brow. He smiled. The smile softened the hard lines of his lean sharp face and made it quite pleasant. Still smiling, he stepped forward, extending both hands.

"Well!" he said smoothly, grasping Tia with one hand and Tony with the other. "Well! It's hard to believe I've finally found you—and after all this time. Tony and Tia! You're both taller than I expected, but of course I forget that young people have a way of growing. I'll bet you can't guess who I am!"

On South Water Street, Tony had learned to classify people by many small signs. It was easy to spot the cheap gamblers, the racketeers, and the little promoters and confidence men. But the few on top belonged to a different breed, and their eyes showed it. Behind the smile, this man's eyes were cold and knowing, with a steely glint that could cut like a drill.

Tony said, "I don't know who you really are, sir. But isn't your name Deranian?"

The man in brown did not change expression. He merely blinked—but it was enough to tell Tony that he had received a shock. Even so, the smile broadened.

"How did you ever guess?" he exclaimed. "Of course my name is Deranian—and so is yours! I'm your Uncle Lucas."

Tony felt Tia's fingers dig into his arm, and he heard her silent whisper of denial.

"My name isn't Deranian," he said stubbornly. "And you're not my uncle."

"Oh, come now, my boy. Don't talk that way. I know this is a surprise—but I am your poor father's brother, and I've had men searching for you for six solid years. I can't imagine how you ever guessed my name when you didn't know your own, though you may have seen a photograph I once sent your father—"

"We weren't guessing!" Tony protested. "Tia knew you right away. You're the man who left us with Granny Malone when we were little."

There were two blinks now, evidence of a really bad shock. Then Mr. Deranian shook his head, looking baffled.

"Son," he said, "you must have me mixed up with your father. But that shouldn't surprise me, considering how much alike we were. It had to be your father who left you with the old lady."

Mrs. Grindley was looking puzzled. "I don't quite understand. The children were so young when it happened—and it's been ten years or more. Do you think either of them would have remembered? It seems impossible. Yet, Tony knew your name."

"Oh, young people," said Mr. Deranian, shrugging and spreading his hands. "Who knows how they know things? In my case maybe it's the family resemblance. Maybe, seeing me, something clicks in his mind." Mr. Deranian snapped his fingers. "Like that. And he remembers. Or maybe he remembers the photograph I sent his father, and the name that goes with it."

He smiled again. "Even though the boy is a bit confused, I think it's wonderful that he remembers what he does. It's further proof of his identity. As for my brother," he went on, "he'd lost his wife, and evidently he'd been employing Mrs. Malone to look after the children. From what we've been able to piece together, it seems that he left them with her when he had to go away on a sudden trip, and that he died before he could get back. One of those tragedies of life."

Mrs. Grindley nodded. "You say you were in Europe at the time?"

"Yes. And you know how it is with brothers. They seldom bother to write, and when they travel a lot it's easy to lose track of each other. I lost track of Paulus, and had no idea he was dead till I returned to America and looked him up. Then I tried to find my niece and nephew. The time I had! It was like hunting for two little needles in a very big haystack. Fortunately I'm not a poor man, or it would have been impossible for me to trace them."

Mr. Deranian produced his silk handkerchief again and wiped his eyes. He smiled at Tia and patted Tony on the shoulder.

"How about it, you two? Would you like to go abroad and live in France for a while with your Uncle Lucas? I've a nice house in southern France; you'd love it there. We can fly over as soon as we get your passports, but they shouldn't take long."

Tony had been listening with astonishment to the man's easy and convincing flow of words. What an operator! he thought. What a smooth-talking, fast-thinking operator! But what's he up to?

He realized suddenly that he and Tia were in a very bad predicament, and that they might need help to get out of it. I'd better call Father O'Day, he thought. Right now, before it's too late.

Mrs. Grindley was saying, "Your niece and nephew don't seem to appreciate what you're doing for them. We'll give them a few days, and maybe they'll wake up. Anyway, it may take longer than you think to get legal custody of them. In a case like this the court would require—"

"Oh, that's all settled," Mr. Deranian hastened to say. "I've been promised custody by tomorrow. You see, my lawyers have been working on this for quite a while. They finally located the children through the welfare office. I was in Rome when they called me about it, and I told them to take it up with the proper authorities immediately. I flew over from Paris yesterday, and got here this morning from New York. So…" He paused, and touched Tony on the shoulder again.

"I don't blame you, young fellow, for being a little balky about accepting me. Fact is, if I were in your place, I expect I would be flabbergasted to discover I had a relative who was going to take me abroad to live with him."

Tony was indeed flabbergasted. Legal custody by tomorrow! He glanced at Tia, and saw the growing fright in her eyes.

"No!" she whispered soundlessly. "I've remembered more about him. We *can't* let him take us!"

FLIGHT

Tony looked despairingly at Mrs. Grindley, wondering if there was any way he could convince her of what was really happening. It seemed impossible. The truth, he realized, just wasn't the sort of thing that most people would believe. Certainly the matron would never accept it.

"Please," he said. "Do we have to go with him just because he says he's kin to us?"

"What's the matter with you?" she snapped, obviously baffled by the way he was acting. "You'll do what the court tells you, and no back talk. You ought to be thankful you have someone who's willing to look after you. Don't you want to live in a decent home—or don't you even realize how lucky you are?"

Tony ran his tongue over dry lips, and tried to get his thoughts in proper order. Suddenly he said, "May I make a phone call, please?"

"To whom?"

"Father O'Day, of St. Paul's Mission."

Her eyebrows went up. "What in the world for?"

"I—I want some advice."

"Advice!" she exclaimed. "Advice about what? About being grateful? About how to treat a relative who has been searching for you for years? Tony, you make me tired."

"I've got a right to call him!" he cried. "No one wants to listen to our side of it, and we need help. He's *not* our uncle, and we can prove it!"

For the first time Mrs. Grindley's square features showed signs of softening. "How?" she asked quietly.

The change in her was so unexpected that Tony floundered a moment. "By—by lots of things," he began. "The fact that we recognized him on sight and remembered his name ought to prove something. Please," he hastened, as Mrs. Grindley started to shake her head. "I know you think it's impossible, but Tia's memory is practically perfect."

"Perfect?" said Mr. Deranian, smiling. "How perfect?"

"She—she can recall everything that happened the day you left us at Granny Malone's. Where you brought us from, what you said, everything." Tony swallowed unhappily. He hadn't wanted to mention Tia's memory, but there seemed to be no way out of it.

There was a curious flicker in Mr. Deranian's eyes. It seemed almost like awe. He believes me, Tony thought. He not only believes me, but he knows something about us, something important.

But almost on the instant Mr. Deranian became his smiling self again. "Wonderful!" he exclaimed, as if he were very much amused by Tia's memory. "And where did I bring you from that day, young lady?"

Tia glanced at Tony, then quickly took a pad of paper from her star box and wrote: *You brought us from a ship.*

"From a ship!" Mr. Deranian echoed. He chuckled and winked at Mrs. Grindley. "So I brought you from a ship! Well, well! It's nice to know my niece has an imagination to go with her memory."

Tony glared at him. "She wrote the truth! And that isn't all. We've learned we have a real relative somewhere, and we're trying to locate him. That's why I've got to call Father O'Day."

Mrs. Grindley said curiously, "What's this about a relative? Does Father O'Day know him?"

"Not exactly, ma'am. But he'll know how to find Sister Amelia— she's the one who got the letter."

"What letter?"

Tony swallowed again. He hadn't wanted to mention Sister Amelia and the meeting at Heron Lake, at least not in front of Mr. Deranian, but there was no way out of it now. He plunged in and told what had happened, and explained about the double star on both the letter and the box.

Mr. Deranian listened intently. Slowly he began shaking his head. "I hate to disappoint you, my boy, but I'm the only close relative you and Tia have. Furthermore, our family has never used the double star as an emblem." He shrugged. "There's no reason why they should. It's a common design on Balkan leatherwork. You'll find it—"

"I don't believe you!" Tony cried. "I want to call Father O'Day. He—"

"Quiet!" Mrs. Grindley ordered. "If there's any phoning to be done, I'll do it myself." She sat back in her chair, frowning from one to the other. "No one's going to be satisfied till we clear this up. And we don't need Father O'Day's help. I happen to know that St. Agnes School is in Baywater. I'll call them direct."

Tony's hopes suddenly rocketed. He watched her pick up the telephone and dial long distance. Presently she was speaking to someone at St. Agnes School and asking for Sister Amelia.

There was a pause while Mrs. Grindley listened. Then she said, "That's too bad. I'm so sorry. When was this?…I see. Well, maybe I had better talk to the Mother Superior. It's about a letter…"

Tony was hardly aware of the rest. All hope had crashed abruptly. Something had happened, and it was worse than Tia had thought. Tia was fighting back tears. Sick at heart, he sank down on the office bench beside her and took her hand.

Mrs. Grindley finally replaced the receiver. "It's too bad," she said. "Sister Amelia has been in poor health for a long time. She was taken to the hospital last week and died the next day. The Mother Superior doesn't know anything about a letter with a star design on it, but she gave me to understand that Sister Amelia may have imagined it. Seems that Sister Amelia's mind has been wandering lately, and that we shouldn't take anything she said too seriously."

Mrs. Grindley frowned at Tony. "I'm really sorry," she said patiently. "But now I think it's time to face facts. I don't know any more about Mr. Deranian than you, but I'm certain the court isn't going to turn you over to him unless he's able to prove he's all right, and that he can give you a good home. As for being your uncle, what real difference does it make what you believe? He's giving you a home, isn't he? A good home is mighty hard to find for young people your age—and especially with your background."

She turned to Mr. Deranian and said, "That poor old nun had them all excited, so of course it was hard for them to accept you. Just give them a chance to think things over. They'll be glad to see you by tomorrow."

Mr. Deranian nodded, smiling. There was something about the smile that, along with the lean face and thin curving lips, the sharp nose and dark hair, suddenly made Tony think of a picture he'd seen of the devil.

Tony could hardly eat his dinner that evening. Afterward, instead of following the others into the main hall to watch television, he went out to the playground with Tia so they could talk alone. He had never felt so discouraged.

Tia whispered, "What are we going to do?"

"I haven't figured it out yet."

"Well, I'm *not* going with him. They can't make me. I'll run away first."

"That's OK with me. Only, I don't know where we'd go. And we can't waste our money."

"But, Tony, we've got *lots* of money. Why don't we just—just take a chance and start south for the mountains?"

He shook his head. "No, that wouldn't be very smart. Anyhow, you heard what the Mother Superior said. Maybe there wasn't any letter after all."

"There *was* a letter! I'm *sure* of it. Tony, I know Sister Amelia wasn't well, but there was nothing wrong with her *thoughts*—not when she talked to us. If she'd been imagining things, there'd have been more to it. Don't you see?"

He considered this a moment, then nodded. Tia might not be practical, but it hardly mattered with the way her brain worked. And if she felt a certain way about a thing, that was the way it was.

Suddenly the future seemed brighter. "O.K. And do you think the letter was written by someone who is really related to us in some way?"

"Of course I do! And, Tony, I believe we can find him."

"How?"

"Sister Amelia gave us a lot to go on. We ought to be able to guess his name."

"Maybe, but that won't take us far. We don't even know what state he's in. Tia, what we need right now is for you to remember more about us. That would be the biggest help in the world."

"Well, I did remember about the ship, and leaving it with Mr. Deranian."

"Go on," he urged.

"There was a cab waiting, and we drove straight out to Granny's.

Only, he made the cab driver take us in. I was so little I could hardly walk. The driver said to Granny, 'These are the kids Mr. Doyle phoned you about,' and he handed her an envelope with fifty dollars in it."

"Who was Doyle?"

"Oh, that was just a name Mr. Deranian gave for himself, so Granny wouldn't know his real name. But I knew his real name because some men on the ship called him that."

"What men, Tia?"

"I can't remember."

"If you think hard, you're bound to remember. Were we on the ship long? And was Mr. Deranian on it with us?"

Tia closed her eyes, then shook her head almost as if she were in pain. "I—I *can't* remember any more. When I go back to that time I—I get all scared and sort of sick."

Tony scowled at the traffic surging past in the deepening twilight. "It's crazy. I can't figure it. A person with a memory like yours just doesn't have it stop cold all of a sudden, at a certain spot, like a tape recorder. There has to be a reason why it stops."

Her small face puckered in thought. "Maybe it's because I don't really want to remember."

"Huh? What's that again?"

"I mean, something awful must have happened, something I wanted to forget. They say that's the way the mind works at times. I was reading about it in one of those reference books in the library." Tia paused, then asked worriedly, "What are we going to do, Tony?"

Tony had already decided what to do, but he did not answer immediately. Swinging slowly past on the sidewalk just beyond the fence was the area policeman following his beat. He could not help eyeing the man distrustfully, for the watchful presence of the law could make things difficult later in the evening.

When the policeman had gone, he said, "We're going to need help to get anywhere. Before we do any traveling I think we'd better talk it over with Father O'Day."

"But—but suppose he makes us come back here?"

"He won't *make* us do anything—he'll just advise us. He's a pretty good guy. I know we can trust him."

They planned to leave for the mission an hour after the lights were out, taking their extra clothes in paper bags. They were going over the details when Winkie appeared.

Tia picked him up. "Oh, Tony," she said earnestly, "what are we going to do about him? We *can't* leave him here!"

"Don't be a dope. How could we ever travel with a cat?"

It was getting dark now. He frowned at the house. "I'll go in first and get some bags from the pantry. Then we'd better slip upstairs and pack 'em while no one's around to ask questions. For Pete's sake, don't try to take everything you've got, or you'll be sorry later."

In the pantry he found two sturdy shopping bags with handles, one of which he gave to Tia. Everyone was still watching television, and they were not noticed as they separated in the main hall and climbed their respective stairways.

In the boys' dormitory he quickly packed his bag with one change of clothing, some extra socks and handkerchiefs and a thin jacket, then hid it in his locker.

It seemed forever before the television program ended and the other boys came upstairs. Presently the last bell sounded. A few minutes later the lights went out.

Tony had made only a pretense of getting undressed. Taking off his sneakers, he stretched out on his cot until he heard Mrs.

Grindley's footsteps on the stairway as she began her final rounds for the night. Now he pulled the sheet over him to hide his clothing, and pretended to be asleep when her flashlight swept the rows of cots.

When she was gone he threw back the sheet and tried to speed the slow minutes by visualizing scenes. But tonight all he could see was the dim face of the clock down in the main hall. The position of the hands suddenly reminded him that, even if they left immediately, it might take them until nearly midnight to travel across the city and reach St. Paul's Mission.

Abruptly he sat up, drew on his sneakers, and eased his bag out of the locker. Very carefully he moved to the stairway, and crept down to the first landing.

The main hall was just below. By the glow of the night light he could clearly see the opposite stairway leading to the girls' dormitory. Tia was waiting on the landing.

Her voice was like a tiny bell in his ear. "I thought you might be early, but we can't leave yet. Mrs. Grindley is in her office, and Miss Devon is fixing a snack for her in the kitchen."

He could hear movements in the distant kitchen. Suddenly light spilled through the house as the pantry door was thrust open. He crouched behind the banisters as the tall figure of the matron's assistant came through the dining room with a tray in her hand, and crossed the main hall. When Miss Devon had vanished in the direction of the office, he whispered to Tia and they tiptoed down the stairs and hastened to the kitchen, where an overhead light still burned. Seconds later they were outside, crossing the service yard to the iron gate, which opened to the alley.

The big iron gate was securely fastened with a padlock. Tia gave it an impatient tug, and the lock snapped open. They began groping through the darkness of the alley toward a distant patch of light marking a side street.

Tony was relieved to find the side street nearly empty at this hour. They turned left here and began to hurry. Three blocks away was a bus stop on a busy avenue.

With the avenue and final freedom in sight, Tony failed to notice the bulky form standing in the shadow of an unlighted doorway. Then the policeman he had seen earlier stepped suddenly in front of them.

"Something after you?" the officer inquired pleasantly. "Or are you just running away from a bad conscience?"

"We—we've got to catch the bus," Tony said, trying to angle around him. "Please, we're late!"

"Not so fast, my friends." The officer held out a restraining hand. "If you're from Hackett House, you're going in the wrong direction." He grinned. "Would you like me to show you the way home?"

Tony was aware that Tia was whispering urgently into her heavy shopping bag. Abruptly a black and furry shape popped out, scrambled across the astounded officer's arm, and went bouncing down the street. It was Winkie.

As Tia raced after the cat, Tony found his wits and cried, "Hurry—catch him!" as he dodged the policeman and ran.

Long minutes later, after reaching another side street through an alley, they came to a bus stop on the avenue. They were safe for the moment, and Winkie was miraculously back in the bag, where he had returned without urging.

No bus was in sight. Rather than risk waiting, Tony hailed the first taxi, and they scrambled inside. Now he looked grimly at Tia's shopping bag.

"Didn't I tell you we *can't* take a cat?" he reminded her. "For Pete's sake, use your head!"

Her chin went up. "Winkie goes where I go."

"This is crazy! A cat isn't like a dog. You can't make him obey. Honestly—"

"He helped us get away, didn't he?"

"That was just an accident. We couldn't possibly carry him on a bus. He'll never—"

"Winkie will do exactly as I tell him," Tia insisted. "He's not an ordinary cat, any more than we are ordinary people."

If she hadn't reminded him how different they were, he would have argued further. But the sudden thought of their many differences held him silent. It was a little frightening to realize their strangeness, and to know that it was probably the cause of all their troubles.

On upper Water Street, before the clicking taxi meter had devoured more than half the five dollars in Tony's pocket, they got out and caught a southbound bus. No one would have suspected Winkie was with them. During the long ride he lay curled in Tia's bag, apparently asleep.

It was well after midnight when they left the bus and hurried across the street to their destination.

St. Paul's Mission was in an old store building near the docks, with a reeking beer parlor on one side, and a pawnshop on the other. It was an unpleasant neighborhood to be caught in at this hour, and Tony was a little jolted to discover that the curtained windows of the mission were dark. He tried the door, and found it locked.

Tia whispered suddenly, "There's a police car coming. If they see us standing here, they—they're sure to stop and ask us questions."

Tony jerked about, his lips compressed. It was a prowl car, all right, and it was moving slowly toward them.

MISSION

There was only one thing to do, and Tia did it on the instant. She grasped the doorknob and turned it with a determined jerk. There was an audible click as the bolt shot back, and the door swung open. She darted inside. Tony followed quickly, then eased the door shut and locked it.

Carefully, through the edge of the glass panel, he watched the prowl car approach close. It stopped directly in front of them. Tony chilled. Had they been seen entering the mission?

For a moment, hiding there behind the door, he had the curious feeling of being caught on a strange planet, where nothing made sense, and everything was a little insane. It was a feeling he had often had before, but never so strongly as now, when the next minute might mean their discovery and possible capture. All at once he realized how much he hated the city; he hated it more than anything on earth, but had never been able to admit it before.

Slowly, the prowl car moved on. Tony expelled a long breath, and turned to study the place they were in.

In the dim light that came through the windows he made out rows of old wooden chairs facing a small rostrum. The room was hot and airless, and smelled of the dirty clothing of the derelicts who wandered in here every night.

A faint hum caught his attention. It was an electric fan. With Tia following, he moved through the gloom to the side of the rostrum, and stopped before a door in the back wall. From under the door came a faint gleam of light.

"Father O'Day!" Tony called. "Are you there?"

There was a grunt, then the scrape of a chair across the floor. Abruptly lights flooded the mission, and the door in front of them was opened.

A big, powerfully built man, collarless and in his shirt sleeves, stood peering down at them in surprise. He was youngish, broad of shoulder, rugged and battered of feature, and wore his wiry black hair in a crew cut—all of which made him look much more like a professional athlete than a priest.

"Is this a visit or a visitation?" he rumbled in a deep bass voice. "In other words, was the street door left unlocked—or did you just materialize from nowhere?"

"The—the door was locked," Tony admitted hesitantly. "But it opened for Tia. I'm sorry to have to bother you so late, Father. Only, we ran away from Hackett House, and we need your help."

The big man blinked at them. "You ran away from Hackett House—and Tia opened the door. Just like that." Suddenly he smiled. "Of course I'll help you! Tell me, can Tia always open locked doors?"

"She doesn't exactly open them, sir. They seem to open for her. If it's right, I mean."

Bushy eyebrows went up. "Honest? You wouldn't kid a fellow?"

"It's the truth, Father. But we'd rather you didn't tell anyone."

"Tell anyone such a tale? And who would believe me?" The rugged face became dreamy for a moment. "Ah, but what a gift! I wish I had it. The things I could do for people…" Then he shook his head. "No, it wouldn't work. If I had such a gift, the devil would be tempting me sure—and confusing me—every minute of the day. He's hard enough to fight now."

Tia asked a question, and Tony said for her, "Tia can't talk, Father, but she wants to know if you really believe in the devil."

"Of course I believe in the devil!" the deep voice said. "Look about you. It took the devil himself to build this part of the city. But don't think of him as a personage. Look upon him as a disease. A sneaky, foul, and dreadful sort of thing. Gets into people's hearts and minds, makes 'em—"

The priest was interrupted by Winkie, who chose this moment to leap from Tia's bag. "Hey there!" he gasped, and immediately scooped Winkie up in his huge hands. "A black cat! Ha! Am I being visited by witches? Don't tell me you brought this fellow all the way from Hackett House in a bag!"

At Tia's nod he stared at the two of them. "Forgive me for ranting about my sworn enemy. He'll just have to keep a bit. You've got problems. Come in here where it's cooler, and let's talk things over."

He turned out the overhead light, and closed the door behind them as they entered the room where the electric fan was going. The place was furnished merely with a cot, some folding chairs, and a desk. Behind a partition, Tony glimpsed a gas stove and a few dishes on a table. Everything was spotlessly clean, and the only luxury was the fan.

Father O'Day shook open some folding chairs for them, then sat down at the desk with the purring Winkie on his lap.

"Let's have it," he began. "You ran away from Hackett House. Why?"

"To—to find our people, and to get away from a man who claims he's our uncle, but who isn't." Tony started with Sister Amelia, then explained at some length about Mr. Deranian. Father O'Day interrupted constantly with surprised questions.

"This beats all," the big priest said at last. "Are you sure, absolutely *sure*, that this man Deranian is the one who left you with Mrs. Malone?"

"Yes, sir. I mean, I'm sure about Tia's memory."

"How about yours? I'd say you were at least a year older than Tia. Can you remember anything yourself?"

"A—a little. Tonight I can remember being brought to Granny's place by a man in a car, after being on a ship. But that's all. It wouldn't have come back to me if Tia hadn't remembered it first."

"What about faces?"

Tony shook his head. "I can't remember a face that far back, when I was so small. Tia can, even though she's younger. She doesn't forget."

"She's forgotten what happened before you were taken from the ship."

"Yes, but she thinks something must have given her a bad shock, so that she doesn't want to remember. Just trying to think about it makes her feel sick."

Father O'Day nodded and looked at Tia. "Probably something did happen; that may be why you can't talk. Now, this man Deranian—"

Tia spoke quickly to Tony, and Tony said, "She's thought of something else. Mr. Deranian was *not* on the ship with us. The captain, or someone in uniform, sent for him after the ship was tied up at the dock, and he came and took us away."

The big man scowled; it made his battered face seem quite ferocious. "Then it looks as if the rascal was paid to take you away. That must be it. There was trouble aboard, and the ship's captain paid him to get rid of you."

"But why would he come back years later and pretend to be our uncle?"

"Well, let's use logic on it. He pretends to be your uncle because he's learned something about you that makes you valuable to him. It's something he didn't know at first."

"He *does* know something," said Tony. "I could tell that when I tried to explain how perfect Tia's memory is. He pretended he didn't believe it, but it gave him a jolt. I—I had the funny sort of feeling that he would have believed almost anything about us—and he's not the kind you can play tricks on."

"Then there's no question that he knows something, and that as your uncle he can profit by it. He seems anxious to get you abroad. Obviously, once he gets you out of the country, no one can question him and he can do what he wants with you. Hmm. What does the fellow look like?"

Tony could not help smiling. "He—he sort of reminds me of your sworn enemy, but without the horns and whiskers."

"You don't mean it!" The priest crossed himself.

"Well, he really does, except that he's clean-shaven. He's pretty sharp-looking—dresses all in brown and spends a lot on his clothes. Why would we be valuable to a man like that?"

"I can think of several reasons." Father O'Day gave another ferocious scowl. He was absently stroking Winkie with one big hand. "Mainly I'd say it has something to do with the fact that you can do things other people can't. I'm presuming that you both have gifts. Only, how could the fellow have learned about you?"

"I don't know," said Tony. "We've never told anyone about ourselves. We—we've always tried to hide things."

"But you must have confided in someone."

Tia shook her head, and Tony said, "Not even Granny. She wanted me to explain to her once how I always knew the time. I tried, but somehow she couldn't understand, and it upset her. Then one evening she caught us making the broom dance...I'll never forget what an awful fright it gave her. I had to lie to her and tell her it was just a trick, and that we were using black threads." He spread his hands. "So you see, we learned pretty early to be careful. If you're too different, people think you're a kook, or even worse."

Father O'Day nodded. "I understand—but *I* don't think there's anything kooky in this. I'd like to know all about what you can do—if you don't mind telling me. Let's start with how you and Tia communicate. It's got me baffled. And what about this time business?"

Tony explained. The big man whistled softly. "What a pair you are! I'd like to know more—you see, I'm terrifically interested in these matters. I believe that people like you and Tia are far ahead of your time. You belong to the future." He paused, and added hopefully, "You mentioned a broom..."

"Wouldn't you rather see our dolls dance? They're not as scary."

"You have dolls that dance? Bless me, by all means!"

Tony smiled. As he reached for his harmonica he wished he had become acquainted with Father O'Day long ago.

The priest sat in wordless delight while magic entered the room and the dolls used his desk for a stage.

"Wonderful!" he whispered finally. "Puppets without strings! After seeing them, I'll skip the broom." He crossed himself. "You know, a whirling broom *would* be rather scary."

"That's why we concentrated on the dolls. When you have to hide it from people, it's safer."

"I can understand that," said Father O'Day. "But I don't understand how you do it. It's a form of telekinesis—do you know what that is?"

Tony nodded. "It's the ability to move things without touching them. Tia has read everything she can find about it. We can both make the dolls dance—but it's much easier when we do it together, and more fun. And of course the music has a lot to do with it."

"Really? In what way?"

"It, well, it sort of amplifies things. I mean, when I play the harmonica, I can move all kinds of heavy objects."

"What a handyman you'd make!" Father O'Day said dreamily. "And do you realize what a problem you've suddenly become?"

Tony sighed. "I imagine it would almost be your duty to send us back to Hackett House. We've sort of put you in a spot, haven't we?"

The priest gave a deep chuckle. "Possibly—but I've been in spots before. The main thing is to keep Deranian from finding you till we figure out some moves. First, to help our planning, let's have some tea and a bite to eat."

They followed him behind the partition, and Tia helped make sandwiches while they waited for the kettle to boil. Presently, with Winkie lapping a saucer of milk in the corner, they sat at the table to eat.

"Food helps make up for sleep," said Father O'Day. "Anyway, I hope you're not too tired, for I think we'd better work out something if it takes till dawn."

"I couldn't sleep now if I tried," Tony admitted.

"Good. Then let's talk about Sister Amelia." The big man glanced at Tia. "Young lady, in spite of what the Mother Superior said, are you still convinced that Sister Amelia received a letter with a double star on it?"

Tia nodded quickly, and Tony said, "If Tia feels certain about something, you can bet it's true."

"Very well. If you believe it, I'll believe it. Without faith we can get nowhere. But I warn you: we'll need a lot of faith to locate an unknown person in an unknown place, in a mountain area that extends for hundreds of miles through several states. Now, what have we to go on?"

At the thought of how little they had, Tony's mouth became grim again. But he said, "We almost have a name. It's not Caroway, Garroway, or Hideaway, but something in between. Hathaway, maybe. Anyway, I'm sure we can guess it. Then we have Tia's memory. If she keeps fishing back, she ought to dredge up something new. And there's her star box."

"Don't forget the money," Tia reminded him.

"Oh, the money!" he exclaimed. "Show it to him, Tia."

"What money?" the priest asked.

"A wad of it she found in her box. The bottom is made of two pieces of leather, and the money was between them all these years."

Father O'Day scowled at the worn folder Tia gave him, then opened it and stared at the money. "Ump!" he rumbled. "That's quite a bundle. I'd like to know what happened on your ship. Tia, have you any idea how long you were on board, or where the ship came from?"

Tia closed her eyes in concentration, then bit her lip. Slowly she shook her head. The priest sighed. "I'm just guessing," he said, "but I've the feeling you were being brought over from abroad somewhere, and that the person bringing you died. Or possibly he was killed. Maybe the captain didn't know what to do with you, and was afraid of an investigation. So he turned you over to his good friend Deranian."

Father O'Day shrugged. "But all that isn't helping us now. The main thing—" He stopped abruptly, frowning at the folder. Then he opened it and thrust the money aside. "This is part of an old road map," he said slowly.

"Yes," said Tony. "But I haven't had a chance to study it."

"Well, it's worth study. It's torn from a larger map, and it shows part of the Blue Ridge area. Maybe it will tell us something."

They bent over the map. Tony's attention was attracted by a thin penciled line following the main highway south from Washington, then branching west to the mountains. It ended in a small town on a secondary road with a circle drawn around it. Beside the circle there was smudged writing that ran to the torn edge. It looked like *Kiált Cast*.

Father O'Day gave a grunt. "Foreign language of some kind. Hmm. Not of the Latin group, but the first word seems almost familiar. The other, well, it may be only part of a word..." He grunted again. "But look at that route. If I were driving my own car down to—" He leaned over the map to read the name of the town marked. "Down to Stony Creek, it is, I'd angle over and take the other route. It's shorter, and you avoid all the heavy traffic and the big cities."

"You've been there?" Tony asked hopefully.

"Not to Stony Creek. It's off the main road. But I've often taken that route to the mountains. I've a friend at a little place called Red Bank; we were on duty together in Vietnam. What I was getting at is this: I don't believe the person who marked the map was thinking of it as a car route."

"Oh!" said Tony, in sudden comprehension. "He planned to travel by bus."

"So it would seem. Of course, the map may mean nothing at all. Possibly it was just a convenient folder to slip the money in. But I don't think so. It's more likely that the map had a special purpose. The person who was bringing you here on a ship may have had it given to him, to show him how to reach his destination."

"I like that better," Tony said instantly. Excitement was suddenly rising in him. "It fits in with everything. I'll bet the man who wrote Sister Amelia lives somewhere near Stony Creek, and that we were on our way there before Mr. Deranian got us."

"Maybe," the priest said. "But we mustn't jump to conclusions. What we need now is time. Stony Creek will have to be investigated, and while that's being done you'll need a safe place to stay."

He slid the money back into the folded map, gave it to Tia, and his big fingers began drumming on the table. A scowl deepened on his battered face, making it quite ferocious again.

Tony asked, "How can we investigate Stony Creek?"

"Oh, there are several ways. Police, church, or some welfare group. If I can get in touch with the right person. But our best bet is Augie Kozak."

"Your friend at Red Bank?"

"Right. I don't think Augie would mind—he has time on his hands. And Stony Creek can't be too far from Red Bank. He could drive over and do some sniffing around—find out if the double star emblem is known to anyone, and check through the local phone book for names on the order of Caroway and Hathaway. But in the meantime…" He began to scowl again.

"What's wrong?"

"I'm trying to think of a safe place for you to hide. I'd rather keep you here—there's space, and extra cots—but I'm afraid it's not safe. Didn't you say you tried to phone me in the afternoon from Hackett House, and that Mrs. Grindley wouldn't let you?"

"Yes, Father."

"Well, that fact will be remembered. Trouble is, there's no good place near that I can send you. Most of the people I know are down-and-outers and drifters, and many of the rest are on the wrong side of the law. But I've something in mind. In the morning I'll do a little phoning and see what can be arranged."

Father O'Day stood up. "I believe we've done all we can for the moment. The next thing is to get some rest. Tony, those cots are in the storeroom yonder. If you'll give me a hand with them…"

In spite of the hour—and it was long past two by the clock Tony visualized—he did not fall asleep immediately. It had been a trying day, and the excitement of the evening was still with him. His mind raced. It touched briefly and uneasily upon Mr. Deranian and then sped on, lured by the promise of Stony Creek. He tried to visualize Stony Creek, but received nothing for his efforts but a blur of darkness broken by a single vague light; he realized he was seeing the place as it was at this moment, and that it was probably so small the streets were unlighted.

Suddenly he remembered how delighted Father O'Day had been with the dancing dolls, and his deep interest in the things Tia and he, Tony, could do. No one else had ever felt that way. Their abilities had seemed unnatural to poor Granny, and any mention of them had upset her. And Granny wasn't the only one. In years past, before they became more careful, others had been upset or even frightened.

All in all, he thought, with the way most people reacted to you, it was a little like being born with too many fingers, or some other defect you felt you ought to hide. So of course they'd hidden the magic—they'd even tried to suppress it until, when they got older, Tia had read all about it and found it wasn't anything to be ashamed of. In fact it was something that, as Father O'Day had said, belonged to the future.

Suddenly, for the first time in his life, Tony wondered what he and Tia could accomplish if they really tried. The possibilities startled him. *What are we?* he wondered. *Where did we come from?*

It was only by a determined effort that he finally made himself go to sleep.

The next thing he knew it was morning, and Tia was shaking him and whispering urgently, "Hurry and get dressed—we've got to leave! Mr. Deranian is outside with a policeman!"

JOURNEY

It was late in the morning and breakfast was on the table, but there was no time for it now. Tony flew into his clothes and caught up his bag. Tia, he saw, was already dressed and ready to leave. She darted past him into the storeroom, urged on by Father O'Day, who was struggling into his coat before his collar was fastened.

"Straight through to the garage," the big man ordered. "Get in the back of the car and crouch down."

In the garage was a small black sedan. Tony scrambled into the rear of it with Tia while the priest unlocked and threw back the door opening into the alley. Seconds later the sedan had swung right into the alley and was racing for the distant cross street.

"They're probably coming on around this way now," Father O'Day muttered. "But I think we have a few seconds to spare. I hate to run—only there's no arguing with a court order, and I'm afraid that's what Deranian has."

"He sure works fast," Tony said unhappily. "Who saw him first?"

"Tia did. Had no idea he was out there, though I was already up and dressed, praise be—save for my coat and collar." The priest was still trying clumsily to fasten his round collar, which had one end adrift in the back. Tony reached up, and with a deft movement of his fingers managed to secure the loose end.

The car slowed momentarily, then whirled into the thin traffic of the cross street. Tia whispered, "I woke up scared, so I knew something was wrong. When I heard someone knocking on the outside door, I peeked through the big room and saw them trying to get in. Mr. Deranian was talking to a policeman, and behind them was another man. I couldn't see very well. There was a green cab waiting for them."

Tony frowned. "Would you recognize the other fellow if you saw him again?"

"I think so. He was wearing a pale-gray suit, and he seemed a lot heavier than Mr. Deranian."

The sedan slowed for a traffic light, stopped for agonizing seconds, then shot forward and whipped around another corner. Father O'Day said quickly, "Tony, sneak a look back, but keep your head down. I saw a cab turning into the far end of the alley before we left it. If it contains our hornless adversary, we may have troubles."

Tony raised up cautiously until he could see the street intersection they had just left. Presently he said, "You're right. It's a green cab, and they're following us."

"Has he still got the policeman with him?"

"He sure has."

The priest made a rumbling sound deep in his chest. "That's not so good. If we shake them, they can stop at any call box, and in two minutes have every police car in the area looking for us. We'll have to pull something out of the bag. Now listen carefully:

"I'm going to step on it and put some distance between us. When I swing around a corner, get ready to jump. I'll stop long enough to let you out. There'll be a drugstore on the corner with a side entrance…Get in there as fast as you can, and stay there till that cab goes by. Got it?"

"Yes, sir. Then you think we should head for the bus station and get tickets for Red Bank?"

There was a startled grunt. "How did you guess?"

"Seems like the most logical move—if your friend Mr. Kozak is willing."

"Don't worry about Augie. They don't come better. I was trying to put through a call to him when that crew behind us interrupted. Anyway, I'll get him on the phone as soon as possible, and tell him to be on the lookout for you. He's a little dark fellow; nice family with two kids. Lives on an apple orchard he owns—place is four miles north of Red Bank on Cahill Road, right on the edge of the mountains."

As he spoke, Father O'Day had been dodging through the traffic, gradually increasing speed. Now suddenly, with a murmured prayer, he ran a red light and raced for the next corner. "Drugstore's ahead," he said. "Get set. Brace yourself as I turn the corner, but don't open the door till I brake. Good luck to you, and phone me if I'm needed—number's Waterview 624-6021. Here we go…"

There was hardly time to thank the big man for his help. Tires squealed as the car took the corner; Tony clung to the seat, then his hand shot to the door handle as he felt the brakes take hold.

In the next breath they were out of the car and running for the safety of the drugstore.

Tony did not think of Winkie until later, when they were in a cab heading for the bus station. With a sudden pang, he glanced at the shopping bag Tia was holding in her lap. It didn't have quite the bulge it had had last night.

"What's the matter?" Tia asked.

"Winkie." Then he added hastily, "Now don't be upset. It's better if he got left behind. You know we couldn't possibly travel with him—he'd get us into more trouble…"

"Oh, Tony, do you really believe that?" She peered at him with a curious look on her small elfin face. "Because if you do, you'd better change your mind. People have to be *very* careful about what they believe. I've read stacks and *stacks* of things about beliefs and believing, and you'd be surprised—"

"Hey, what's the lecture about?"

"Winkie, of course. I told you he was a very special cat, and you've got to believe it. Who do you think woke me up this morning?"

"You telling me Winkie woke you up?"

"Of course! If he'd been a minute later... Anyway, I woke up scared because of him, and thank goodness I put on my good slacks instead of that worn-out dress. I had a feeling we'd be going on a trip." She stopped, wrinkled her nose at him, then whispered into her bag. There was a faint meow, and Winkie thrust his sleek black head into sight.

Tony groaned. Suddenly he said, "But your bag—you must have left something behind."

"I left that horrid old dress behind. Mrs. Grindley wouldn't let us wear slacks, you know. Just dresses. The one I was wearing came out of donations. I hated it."

"Well, you sure look better now," he conceded. "Especially for going places. And before I forget it, you'd better give me some of that money so I can buy tickets."

As they entered the crowded bus station, Tony felt the sudden rise of an excitement he had never known before. They were about to continue a journey that had really started long ago. A journey that had been strangely interrupted, that even now someone was trying to prevent. There was no imagining what lay behind it all, but Stony Creek should furnish some answers...

Standing in line for tickets, he was momentarily dismayed to find himself under the watchful scrutiny of a policeman. On the chance that he might be remembered, he bought tickets for Washington instead of Red Bank. They were going through Washington anyway, and he could get tickets for the rest of the journey there.

They had nearly an hour to wait, a matter that worried him and kept him constantly on watch, though it gave them time to clean up and have something to eat in the adjoining restaurant. In the continual rush about them no one seemed to notice the small black cat on the floor between Tia's feet, quietly nibbling a hamburger she had given him.

Tony was vastly relieved when they were finally aboard their bus and headed out of the city. The bus was packed and he was unable to sit with Tia, but at the moment it didn't matter. The excitement had come back. They were on their way, and no one was going to stop them.

By the time they reached Washington Tony had decided they'd better cover their trail a little more carefully. For anyone as fast-moving and resourceful as Mr. Deranian, it would be foolish to leave any clue to their destination. After a quick study of the map, he bought tickets for Fairview, the first town east of Red Bank. When they got there tomorrow, he could phone Augie Kozak to come and get them.

Again there was a long wait, but on the new bus he was able to sit with Tia. He had been wanting to talk things over with her for hours; now, though, he hardly knew where to begin, and he could feel weariness finally catching up with him.

For a while he dozed. When they were well on their way to Richmond, he shook himself awake and frowned down at Tia's bag. Winkie was still curled in it asleep.

"I told you not to worry about him," Tia reminded him. "He'll be all right till we change buses again."

They would change buses, he remembered, late that night at a place called Winston-Salem.

"We've a lot to figure out," he began. "Have you been able to remember anything else?"

"Not yet. But, Tony, I believe we can figure *some* things out if we just start at the right place."

"Where's that?"

"With us."

"Huh?" He frowned at her.

"That's right, with *us*. Tony, what *are* we? Have you any idea at all?"

He shook his head. "I was wondering the same thing last night."

"Well, I've been thinking…"

"Let's have it."

"Tony, it's only half an idea, mainly something I *feel*. It's hard to put it into *words*. But it's something I've always felt a little—because of our being so different, I mean—only I didn't like to face it. I suppose for a long time I hated to *admit* we were different."

"I know what you mean. When you're the way we are, people make you afraid to be yourself. And most people want to be like everybody else. If we could only live in a place where everyone expects you to be different…"

"We will, Tony. I'm *sure* that's the sort of place we're going to."

"We'll have to find it first," he muttered. "And that's no answer to what we are."

"It *is* in a way!" she insisted. "Don't you see? If there are more people as different as we are, then, well—maybe we're members of a different *race* of people. Sort of like the Gypsies."

"Could be," he admitted. "Only I wish we had a little more to go on."

"Oh, we have! Don't you remember what Sister Amelia said was in the letter she got?"

"How do you mean?"

"She said the man who wrote it wanted information about certain *unusual aptitudes* in her pupils. And that it was for some kind of research he was doing."

"Certain unusual aptitudes?" He blinked at her. "I'd almost forgotten that."

He considered it a while, and suddenly exclaimed, "Say, that sounds as if he was really searching for people like us. Only he was being careful about it, so it wouldn't cause too much attention."

"Tony," she replied slowly, "I believe he was searching for *us*. If he was, then it proves that we didn't just *happen*. I mean, like being born with red hair in a family where everyone's hair was dark. You see, we were so little when we were brought to Granny's, and no one could even have *guessed* what we'd be like later—unless we came from people where everyone is *expected* to be different in all sorts of ways."

She paused, then added, "So I say we came from a different *race* of people, like the Gypsies, and that we got lost from them, and that man who wrote Sister Amelia was looking for us."

Maybe it was sort of far out, but it did make sense. He looked at her with a new respect. Most of the time she was only a timid and much-too-sensitive kid sister who had to be protected. But at other times, like now, she was miles ahead of him.

Gypsies, he thought. Maybe so. The double star on the letter and the box proved something, as did the map with the money in it, and the marked bus route—the route that ended at Stony Creek, which surely must be near the Blue Ridge area where the letter had come from.

Tony squirmed in the bus seat, then closed his eyes and concentrated on Stony Creek. This time it came clear. It wasn't much to look at—a row of shops and a filling station, and a bridge over a rushing stream. Abruptly he changed his mind and decided it was something to look at, because the stream was so clear you could see the pebbles in the bottom, and it was wonderful to watch it coming down over the rocks, making a series of white cascades under the crowding trees. The few cars in sight looked expensive, and he decided that their owners must have summer homes somewhere near.

It was the sort of place you could dream about—but, what were Tia's Gypsies doing there?

"Tia," he said, "let's go back to the ship again. Before Mr. Deranian came. There *must* be something…"

"But, Tony, I've told you everything I can."

"You only think you have," he insisted. "If I keep asking questions, something's bound to come back."

"I'm so tired. We didn't get much sleep last night, and I can hardly keep my eyes open now. If we have to change buses tonight, we may not get any sleep at all."

"Well, O.K. Maybe we'd better get some rest."

They adjusted their seats and lay back with their eyes closed. Tony drifted off; he must have slept for a while, because when he opened his eyes again, the scene outside had changed. Instead of the continual works of man, he was glimpsing the first real rural country he had ever seen. Heron Lake hadn't prepared him for anything like this.

Reluctantly he turned his attention to Tia when he heard her sudden whisper.

"Tony, I've just remembered something."

"Huh? What?"

"Tony, we spoke another language when we first came to live with Granny."

He looked at her incredulously. "You're kidding!"

"It's true," she insisted. "I didn't realize it before; that may be why it's been so hard to remember about the ship."

"Any idea what the language was?"

"No, except it was *very* different from English. We seem to have known a little English too, but we didn't *think* in English like we do now."

"What language did the people on the ship speak?"

"I—I'm not sure. It may have been Spanish part of the time, though I'm just guessing. I believe the captain spoke English—at least to us."

"No one spoke the other language?"

"Someone did. I—I—" She faltered, and her face twisted as if she were in pain. Then she whispered, "Uncle Bené spoke it."

Tony held his breath. Quietly he asked, "Who was Uncle Bené?"

"I—I—" Tears sprang to Tia's eyes, and she began to tremble. Suddenly she put her hands over her face. "I—I think he died," she whispered. "Please—please don't ask me any more. Not now."

"O.K."

Uncle Bené. He began repeating the name over and over in his mind. It was like a tiny glow far away in the darkness of yesterday. When he was little there'd been someone he'd called Uncle Bené; someone who, for a short time, had been very important to him. The name had meant comfort and safety in a time of terror.

He was still trying to recall the person who went with the name when they rolled into another station for a dinner stop that evening.

Tia said little while they ate. Her small face was pinched, and in her eyes was the shadowed fear that always came when memory groped too far.

Later, on the bus, he said, "Stop worrying about Uncle Bené. He'll come back to us both if we don't try too hard."

"I can't help it," she told him. "The things that happened to us are beginning to seem so close—so close I can almost see them. Only, I—I can't make myself look at them."

"Forget about it till tomorrow. Let's think about us again." He frowned. "I've been wondering where Mr. Deranian could have learned anything about us. Whatever he knows, he must have picked it up recently. But who from?"

"I think he got it from someone abroad," said Tia. "And I'll bet he's being paid to take us back."

"Well, he'll never catch us."

"I'd feel better if we knew what he was doing now. Tony, can't you *see* him?"

"You know I can't see people the way I can places. Anyhow, it's dark."

"You can *try*. Tony, if we just practiced more and really *tried*, I'm sure we could do all *sorts* of things we never thought of."

"Yeah, I think you're right."

He closed his eyes and concentrated on Mr. Deranian. "I see a city," he said presently. "A city street with a lot of traffic. It could be Washington, but I'm not sure. If Mr. Deranian's there, I can't see him. There are so many people…"

While the bus sped on through the night, he tried again and again. But the pictures became dimmer, and all he learned was that the city was Washington, for once he had a vague glimpse of the Capitol.

Had Lucas Deranian actually traced them as far as Washington?

He fell into a troubled sleep finally. When he awakened it was nearly three in the morning, and they were entering Winston-Salem, where they were to change buses for Fairview.

Their next bus did not leave until long after daylight. Winkie accounted for part of the wait by scampering off in an alley after they fed him a hamburger outside. Later, in the nearly empty station with Winkie back in Tia's bag, they curled on a bench to get what rest they could. Unfortunately they were seen entering the station by a policeman who had not been around when they arrived.

The officer was pleasant, but he insisted upon knowing where they had come from.

"Washington," said Tony, figuring that half the truth was all that safety would permit. "We got here on the last bus."

"Oh? And where are you going?"

"Fairview."

"I see. You live in Fairview?"

"No, sir. We're just going to visit some of our people." Tony was wide awake and worried by now, though he was pretending to be half asleep. The policeman jotted something in his notebook. "What's your name, young fellow?"

"Castaway." Why he said it, Tony didn't know. It just slid off his lips in place of Malone, which wasn't his real name after all. He saw Tia give him a startled and almost frightened look.

"Castaway," the officer repeated. "I never heard that one before. If you are going to Fairview, you must have tickets. May I see them, please?"

At the sight of their tickets the officer was satisfied.

"O.K., son. Sorry to bother you, but there are lots of young people on the loose these days, getting into trouble. When things get too hot, they think they can cool off in a bus station without being noticed." He saw Winkie peering at him from Tia's bag, and suddenly grinned. "What d'you know! Traveling with a black cat! Better not let the bus driver see it."

This brush with authority was unsettling, and there was no sleep for them until they at last went aboard their bus. It was old, and the seats were uncomfortable, but by this time they were too weary to care.

Late in the morning Tony was awakened by Winkie crawling into his lap. He sat up abruptly and looked at Tia, whose eyes were worried.

"He won't stay in the bag," she told him. "Fairview's the next stop. I—I'm afraid something's wrong. I wish we'd gotten off before…"

He glanced quickly out of the window and saw that they were entering a town. It was a squalid and almost treeless little place, with a few old stores, a scattering of run-down houses, and an auto junkyard. Slowing, the bus turned off the highway and braked before one of the stores, which apparently served as a station. Several people stood waiting out front.

"Fairview," called the driver, opening the door.

Uneasy, Tony got their bags and followed a woman and a child outside. Behind him came Tia, clinging tightly to Winkie.

In front of the store he paused uncertainly, suddenly conscious of the silence about him, of the people watching them curiously. Then someone touched him on the shoulder, and he turned to see a short, red-faced man with a badge pinned to the pocket of his sweaty shirt.

"You looking for anyone, son?"

"I only wanted to find a telephone," said Tony.

"Well, if you'll come along quiet, an' don't give me no trouble, I might let you use the one at the police station."

"Police station!" Tony exclaimed.

"That's right, son. I'm Chief Purdy. I know who you are, an' I got orders out of Washington to hold you."

JAIL BREAK

Tony looked incredulously at the short man. A cold knot was gathering in his stomach.

"W-what's this all about?" he stammered.

"Son, if your name's Malone, alias Castaway," Chief Purdy told him, "you ought to know what it's all about. An' don't tell me you ain't the right pair. You're the only young folks on the bus, and the description fits you perfect. Even to the black cat." He smiled thinly, showing tobacco-stained teeth. "Now, if you'll just come along..."

"Just a minute, Ben," said a gaunt man in overalls. "What you going to do with the girl? She looks kinda young to be locked up."

"I don't know how old she is, Milt, but from what they tell me about her it won't be the first time she's been in the pokey. But if you an' May want to be responsible for her till they send somebody to pick 'em up..."

A gray-haired woman shook her head quickly and whispered to the gaunt man, "Stay out of it, Milt. I wouldn't have that foxy-faced girl in the house."

Tony said desperately, "You're making an awful mistake! Who was it in Washington told you—"

"Don't argue, son," the short man said patiently. "We'll talk it over at the station."

Tony winced as a square, powerful hand closed over his elbow and began to guide him down the street. The opposite hand had Tia by the elbow. They moved past the junkyard, and over to a filling station where two scrawny bears stood watching in a cage. As they turned past the cage, Tony heard the bears give little wistful grunts to Tia's silent whisper of greeting. Then Tia said, "Look, Tony, look!" and he raised his head and saw the mountains for the first time.

They were so unexpectedly close, so wonderfully green and blue and strange, that they quite took his breath away. Involuntarily he stopped and stared.

The short man thrust him on. "What's the matter with you, son?"

"The mountains…"

"Pshaw, ain't you never seen mountains before?"

"Not close like this."

"Well, they ain't nothin' to get excited over. But the tourists like 'em. Mountains an' bears. That's why I keep them bears. They attract tourists to the gas station."

Because he suddenly hated the man, Tony could not help saying, "Don't you ever feed them? They look hungry."

"Pshaw, fool bears." The chief spat, showing his first sign of irritation, and propelled them across the rear of the lot to a small, dilapidated block building with the words FAIRVIEW POLICE crudely painted over the door. As they approached it, Winkie leaped nervously from Tia's grasp and vanished in the surrounding weeds.

Inside, beyond a scarred desk, some radio equipment and a few broken chairs, Tony glimpsed a partially open door that shut off a small area containing two cells. The place was unpleasantly hot and dirty.

The short man nodded at the desk. "Phone's there. But first, I'm wondering who you're aiming to talk to around here."

"Nobody. I want to call long distance."

"I'm not sure I can let you do that, son." The chief shook his head, and rubbed his hand over his knotty red face. He was a deliberate person, with a thin, wide mouth that kept moving slowly as if he were chewing something. Tony, looking at him angrily, visioned the ill-fed bears, and thought: You dirty old penny pincher...

"But I've a right to make a call," he protested. "And you've no right to arrest us like this!"

"Now don't get het up, son. I don't like to arrest young people, but sometimes it's my duty. When you get in trouble you got to take your punishment—an' from what I hear you're in plenty trouble." The chief glanced at the doorway as the gaunt man in overalls appeared. "Milt," he went on, "this young feller wants to make a long-distance call. You're the mayor. What d'you think?"

"If I remember the law, Ben, he's allowed to make one call. So, if he's got the money to pay for it..."

"I have the money," Tony said quickly.

"Not so fast," said the chief. "There's a sort of complication, Milt. I didn't want to mention it outside, but Washington's paying a reward for this pair."

"Eh? How much?"

"One thousand dollars."

Tony sucked in his breath, and he heard the mayor whistle softly. Would Lucas Deranian actually pay that much to catch them? But of course he would. After all that had happened there was no question of it. Yet it was a shock to suddenly realize how very much the man wanted them, and the steps he would take to find them.

"That sort of changes things," the gaunt man in overalls said slowly. "If they're wanted that bad, it sounds as if they're mixed up in something pretty big. All it would take is one call out of here to the right person, an' first thing you know they'd have a lawyer here with a writ, an' you'd have to release them."

Tony glared from one to the other. "Does that mean you're not going to let me make my phone call?" he demanded.

The short man nodded, and said quietly, "That's right, son. If they want to let you make phone calls in Washington, that's their business. My duty is to keep you here till the deputy comes to get you."

"You're not thinking about your duty," Tony retorted angrily. "All you care about is that thousand dollars. And you're making a mistake, because the person who's paying it—"

"That's enough out o' you, son." The short man's voice was still mild, but there was a narrowing of the eyes and a thinning of the mouth that warned Tony of the uselessness of saying more.

He had wanted to call Father O'Day, but now he realized it had been mainly for the assurance of hearing the voice of the only friend he and Tia had. Actually, there was nothing Father O'Day could do, except to inform Augie Kozak of what had happened. They were on their own here. The only wise thing was to stop arguing, and take it easy until tonight. Then they could slip out and head for the Kozak place.

They'd had little rest for two nights, and Tia, he saw, was drooping with fatigue. Even so, he was not surprised to find that she seemed oblivious of their predicament, and that all her attention was on the distant bear cage. She was watching it through the window and whispering silently, "You poor things! But just wait— I'll get you out of there."

"Don't be a dope," he cautioned her in the same quiet voice. "We won't have time to worry about bears when we leave here. Don't you realize the spot we're in?"

Her only answer was a stubborn lifting of her chin. Oh, he thought, on top of everything else, we've got *bears* to think about...

"Ben," the man in overalls was saying, "what's the story on these two? Did Washington call you direct?"

"Yeah, but I got word from Winston-Salem first. Lemme lock 'em up an' I'll tell you about it."

Tony made no protest as they were searched, but he asked if he could keep his harmonica. The request was denied, and all their possessions were locked in a cabinet behind the desk. Then they were hustled past the corridor door and each thrust into a cell.

Feeling lost without his harmonica, he peered about him in disgust. The place was filthy, but at least it had an upper bunk that seemed a trifle less dirty than the lower one. He swung wearily up to it and stretched out, and could have fallen asleep instantly if he had not heard Ben Purdy talking.

The chief had lowered his voice, but it was easy for Tony to hear him even with the corridor door closed.

"It was like this, Milt. First, Winston-Salem got a call from Washington to be on the lookout for this pair at their bus station. One of their cops remembered seeing 'em early this morning, only they gave their name as Castaway instead of Malone. They had tickets for here. So right off Winston-Salem tells Washington about it, then they call me. I'd no sooner got through talking to 'em when Washington calls me direct."

"But, Ben, who was it in Washington called you?"

"Feller named Karman. Werner Karman. He's some kind of deputy in the Treasury Department."

"*Treasury* Department?"

"That's right. He said to grab those kids an' lock 'em up fast, and don't take no chances with 'em. I asked was they armed, and he said no but the boy's known to be dangerous an' likely the girl is too. He said they both got police records, an' on top of it they escaped from some sort of correctional institution up north."

"I wouldn't have believed it," came the mayor's voice. "And I'd hardly say they look dangerous. Why, the boy didn't even have a knife in his pocket."

"You can't go by looks, Milt. To look at 'em, you wouldn't think the Government wanted 'em, and that the Treasury Department would be offering a big reward."

"Seems kinda odd, Ben. Sure it's the Treasury Department paying the money?"

"Well, who else would it be?"

"Didn't you ask?"

"Pshaw, when a feller says he's bringing me a thousand dollars cash for doing my duty, I ain't askin' whose pocket it come out of. I did ask what the kids had done, an' he let on it was pretty hush-hush, an' that Washington wanted 'em for questioning, an' wanted 'em fast. So I told him O.K., an' should I call 'im back when I got his prisoners locked up safe. An' he said don't bother, that he knew I'd have 'em when he got here, that he was in a hurry to catch a plane so he could get here before dark. He's flying to Winston-Salem, then renting a car."

"Hmm. He sure wants those kids bad."

Tony suddenly chilled with apprehension.

"Tia," he called silently, "did you hear all that?"

"Hear what?" she replied. "I wasn't paying any attention. Tony, there's a little barred window high up on the wall here, and from the top bunk I can look out and see the mountains! Oh, Tony they're *beautiful!* If there's a window in your place—"

He groaned. "For Pete's sake, listen to me," he begged. "Tia, Mr.

Deranian is on his way from Washington now to get us. We can't wait till dark to get out of here. We'll have to do it this afternoon."

"Oh, dear. Let's not worry about it. If we've *got* to do it, we'll do it. Tony, why do people have such *awful* places as this to lock other people in?"

"It's because they're people. They're no better here than they are on South Water Street."

"Tony—"

"Hush—they're talking again."

The mayor was saying, "It's a funny deal, Ben. You reckon we ought to call Washington and do a little checking on this Karman?"

"Don't see why. He'll have to show me his badge an' papers before I release any prisoners to 'im—*and* the money. He said he'd bring it with him in cash. So, for *that* much money…"

"You'll have to split it with Winston-Salem."

"No, I don't. Wasn't nothing said about that. You'll get your cut, like as always."

"Well, I'm not one to argue with cash. But I do say there's something queer about the deal."

"There could be. Fact is, just before he hung up, Karman said, 'Be careful with those kids, or they'll get away from you. Don't let 'em out of your sight till I get there.' Pshaw, they couldn't get away—not through two locked doors."

There was a short silence. Then the mayor said, "I think he was warning you, Ben, that they're not ordinary kids. You can tell that by looking at them. Any idea why they came to Fairview?"

"No. I been wondering about that myself. I thought the boy was going to ask to phone somebody in town, but he fooled me."

"There's got to be a reason why he's here. Ben, I think we ought to ask him a few questions."

"So do I. I'll go get 'im."

Tony, worried about how they were going to slip away safely in daylight, was suddenly glad of the chance to see the office again. Then, too, there was his harmonica. Without it he felt like Samson shorn. Somehow he had to get it back, for he might need it later in an emergency.

As he sat down in one of the broken chairs, the short man studied him a moment, then said, "You know anybody here in Fairview, son?"

Tony shook his head.

"Then why did you an' your sister come here?"

"Because we wanted to."

"That ain't answering my question, son."

"It sounds like a good answer to me. May I have my harmonica back, please?"

"Afraid not, son. There's got to be a reason why young folks travel so far to a strange town. 'Course we know you're running away from the law, but it don't make sense to come to a place like this unless you know somebody around here."

"Or was planning to meet someone," added the mayor.

"Please," said Tony again, "may I have my harmonica?"

"I done said no," the chief replied irritably. "Now I want some straight answers, son, an' I want them quick. Y'hear me?"

"You've no right to ask me questions, and I don't have to answer them. But if you'll give me my harmonica I'll tell you the truth— only I know you won't believe it."

The chief regarded him a moment in angry silence. Then the mayor growled, "Aw, give 'im the fool thing, Ben. He ain't likely to hurt nobody with it."

The short man unlocked the cabinet, took out the harmonica,

and began turning it slowly in his square hands as if he expected to find that it was really a deadly weapon in disguise. Finally he blew upon it before he tossed it to Tony.

Tony wiped it carefully on his sleeve, and placed it to his lips. In the corner behind the two men he saw an umbrella and a broken-down broom; and near them a raincoat hanging on a hook. With his eye on the broom he breathed lightly into the harmonica, and saw the broom handle rise a few inches beside the raincoat. He allowed it to settle back into place, and in turn moved an ashtray on the desk and a small pebble beyond the open door. He could have shifted all these objects without the aid of the harmonica, but somehow the music seemed to give him power. With its help he'd sometimes felt he could move great weights he couldn't have budged with his bare hands.

Ben Purdy said impatiently, "Come on, boy; I'm waitin' to hear you talk."

Tony slid the harmonica into his pocket. "All right, but I said you won't believe it. Tia and I are running away from a man who says he's our uncle, but who isn't. His name is Deranian. He's got a man helping him—I don't know who he is, but he may be the one you talked to in Washington, who calls himself Karman. The reason we came here is because we've a relative living down here some-where. We're not sure of his name, but it's something like Caroway, or Castaway." Tony stopped and wearily rubbed his hands over his face. He was so tired it was becoming hard to keep his eyes open. "That's about all," he added, "except that the Government doesn't want us for anything."

The men looked at him silently for a moment, then glanced at each other. Finally the short man spat irritably on the floor. "Pshaw, anybody could tell a better one than that. If you're so innocent, how come they're paying a big reward for you?"

"And not only that," said the mayor, "but if Washington doesn't want you, how'd you happen to know about Karman? I'm sure, young feller, we never spoke that name in front of you."

"I heard you talking about him after you locked us up."

"Not through that closed door you didn't."

Tony shrugged. "My hearing's better than you think."

Ben Purdy said, "We're tired o' lies. You gonna answer our questions, boy?"

"I've answered them."

"What you need is a good licking. I got a mind—"

"Easy, Ben," the mayor cautioned him. "You know the law. Better lock 'im up and let Washington worry about 'im."

Back in his cell, Tony climbed to the upper bunk again and peered out of the narrow barred window. Since the window faced the west, the direction they would have to take to reach the Kozak place, his only interest at the moment was to pick an escape route. But he had not counted on seeing, for the first time in his life, a vast sweep of country that spread before him like a great beautiful park.

He gaped. Ahead were rolling pastures and mounting green hills that rose higher and higher until they merged into a shimmering curtain of blue that topped the clouds. It was a strange and marvelous world, and he wanted suddenly to get out in it and feel the grass under his feet, and smell and touch and know the wonder of it all.

Then he remembered what he had to do, and tried to fix in his mind the easiest way over the hills. Looking closer, he realized the police station was on the edge of a hill, for below him the ground dropped away to a brushy ravine with a creek at the bottom. To get away, they would have to cross that creek and climb to what seemed to be a field of corn on the other side of the ravine.

Finally he lay back and closed his eyes.

It seemed he had hardly gone to sleep before someone was shaking him awake. He rolled over and saw Ben Purdy.

"Get up, boy. It's time we had a little talk."

Tony chilled as a square hand closed like a vise around his wrist and he was hauled into the office. He realized unhappily that it was late in the afternoon, and that he had slept far longer than he had intended. If only he'd woken up earlier, he and Tia might be hurrying over the hills by now. For surely there must have been moments when Ben Purdy was away from the place…

"Like I said earlier," the short man began, "what you need is a good licking." He took something from a desk drawer and slapped it lightly across his hand. It was a short piece of rubber tubing. "Now, son, I want an answer to them questions we asked you earlier."

Tony ran his tongue over dry lips. The time had come to leave, but how was he going to manage it? He glanced at the outer door. It was closed, and probably locked. But the window beside it was open and he could see the pebbles and debris in the lot outside.

Suddenly he called to Tia, then drew his harmonica from his pocket. At the first note a pebble rose from the path and shot toward the window. He directed it poorly and it flew too high and smashed the glass. Even so, it had the desired effect of diverting the chief's attention.

Lips compressed, Ben Purdy turned quickly to the window and looked out. Muttering, he spun about at a sound behind him, and stiffened as he saw Tia hurrying from the cell area.

"How—how'd you get in here?" the chief said hoarsely. "So help me, get back in there where you belong!"

Tia ignored him and ran across the room, following Tony's orders. She jerked open the outer door, then darted to the cabinet where their things were locked. Ben Purdy tried to catch her, but the ashtray rose threateningly from the desk and struck him, and he found his way barred by the broom and the raincoat, which were no longer where they had been. The broom was suddenly clothed by the raincoat, which waved its empty sleeves as if invisible arms were inside.

In Ben Purdy's paling face anger and disbelief were swiftly giving way to panic. Abruptly he lunged to the desk and tried to pull open one of the drawers. Guessing he was after a weapon, Tony blew a shuddering darkness into the harmonica; from it poured a wildness and a wailing, a terrible beat of sound that sent the raincoated broom leaping and whirling around the desk like something possessed. It became a live thing, a thing of madness, a whirling scourge that tore about the place scattering everything before it. The short man retreated from it in horror until he was forced into a corner. He cringed there, petrified.

Tia, with her bag and star box, ran outside. Swiftly Tony got his own things from the cabinet and started to follow. On the threshold he stopped, for Tia was not going where he had told her. She was racing for the bear cage.

"Hey!" he called in dismay. "There isn't time!"

"I've *got* to free them," she flung at him. "*No* one has *any right* to lock up poor animals and treat them so horribly. Hold that awful man back a little longer."

Reluctantly, Tony sent the broom and the raincoat whirling again on their ghoulish dance.

The gray-faced man in the corner stared at him with stricken eyes. He managed to gasp, "You—you two ain't human. Wha—what are you?" He gulped and spat hoarsely, "*Witches!* That's what you are—*witches!*"

Tony groaned inwardly. We've really cooked it this time, he thought. Nothing, he realized, would ever be the same for Tia and himself again. What they'd done here today would be told over and over again, for all the world to hear.

He glanced in the direction of the bear cage, and abruptly caught up his bag and ran.

THE BEARS

The freeing of the bears was causing a much greater commotion than Tony had counted on. Two cars full of summer tourists had stopped at the filling station, and a half dozen people were approaching the cage as Tia reached it and began tugging at the rusty padlocks on the door.

The attendant saw her and yelled, but Tia paid no attention to him. When the door came open, tourists scattered. Women screamed. In seconds there was a traffic jam in front of the station as drivers braked to gawk at two momentarily bewildered black bears being urged away by a thin girl with pale hair. Then awkwardly but swiftly, one on either side of her, the bears began to run for the brushy ravine at the edge of town.

Tony waited at the far corner of the police station until Tia was safely down the slope before he pocketed his harmonica and hastened after her. Long before he reached the muddy creek at the bottom he was aware of rising excitement in the town. Men were running, calling to each other, questioning, and twice he heard Ben Purdy's voice, hoarsely trying to explain what had happened.

He lost sight of Tia in the brush, but found her waiting uncertainly by the creek. Beyond her the bears were standing half submerged in midstream, drinking thirstily while they cooled off. Winkie sat watching on the bank.

"Which way do we go, Tony?"

"Follow the creek," he told her. "A little farther on we'll have to cross it and climb to a cornfield. Get going—they may be starting after us soon!"

He didn't think Ben Purdy would be in a great hurry to follow them; unless, of course, he got someone to help. But you never could tell. Money was everything to some people, and a portion of the reward was enough to make even the mayor overlook a few points.

There was a faint trail bordering the creek, apparently made by fishermen. They were racing along it when he heard sounds behind them. Glancing back, he saw the two bears approaching.

"Do we have to have those—those *friends* of yours with us?" he panted.

"They won't bother you," Tia assured him.

"Don't be a dope! Bears are bears! Who said they won't bother us?"

"*They* did, of course."

"Huh? Since when could you understand bear talk?"

"It's simple enough, Tony. If you have any *real* feeling for animals, you know exactly how *they* feel, and that's practically the same as being able to *talk* to them. Can't you see they love us?"

"No, I can't," he muttered. It was all right for Tia to be that way—she could probably get along fine with a man-eating tiger. But he wasn't Tia.

The creek widened in a stony area; Tony stopped to study it, and saw the bears wheel and splash across through the shallows. It was as if they knew this was the best way to the cornfield. Quickly he drew off his shoes and socks and followed. Tia waded behind him, carrying Winkie. The creek felt wonderfully cool to their feet. As there was still no sign of pursuit, they paused briefly at the farther bank to bathe their hot faces and gulp satisfying draughts of the muddy water. Tia commented that they probably would die of typhoid. "But it sure *tastes* good," she added. "If we only had something to *eat*...Tony, didn't you buy some candy bars this morning?"

"Yeah, but we'd better save 'em till later. We can't reach Kozak's place tonight. It's too far. Anyhow, it looks as if it might rain soon. Let's get going—we've got to find a place to keep dry."

The bears, he saw, had vanished up a long gully leading out of the ravine. He led the way upward through the brush and they came out at a corner of the cornfield. Here the big, gaunt animals had pulled down several stalks and were happily feeding on the yellow ears.

With an uneasy glance at them, Tony turned left and began hurrying along the edge of the field. Ahead, over the crest of the hill, he could see dark clouds that now hid the mountains and the lowering sun. Even so, the heat seemed almost worse than it had been all day.

"Do you suppose raw corn would hurt us?" Tia said. "I'm so *hungry.*"

He plucked two ears and shucked them, and they nibbled at them experimentally as they hastened over the hill. They hadn't eaten since daylight and he was surprised to discover how good the fresh kernels tasted. Before they left the field, he plucked several more ears to carry with them.

On the other side of the hill they scrambled through a strip of woods, and suddenly found their way barred by a barbed wire fence. Directly ahead, across a pasture full of grazing cattle, was a cluster of farm buildings and a barn lot where men were at work.

In his ignorance of the country Tony hadn't counted on such obstacles as farmyards, and pastures of cattle with uncertain dispositions to force him from his course. To reach a safe area and avoid being seen, they had to circle entirely around the farm. By this time all the sky had darkened and thunder was beginning to roll ominously overhead.

They reached another barbed wire fence, crawled under it, and were hurrying across the narrow field beyond when the first cold drops began to fall. Abruptly lightning split the sky. Tia had been carrying Winkie, and now the little cat leaped from her grasp and streaked away in fright. Tony looked wildly around for some sign of shelter, but saw only the patch of woods ahead. He began to run.

"This way!" Tia cried. "Follow Winkie!"

They raced around the edge of the woods where the pasture curved. Winkie must have been able to smell a mouse haven, for tucked in the corner at the far end of the pasture was a small hay barn.

They barely managed to reach it before the black skies opened and a fury of driving rain hid the world around them.

It was still pouring when darkness came, but Tony did not mind. They'd eaten the rest of the corn and a candy bar apiece, and finally they'd burrowed comfortably down into the warmth of the hay, for it had turned surprisingly cold after so much heat.

He had lost all sense of direction, and in the intense darkness he could not even see Tia a few feet away. Despite the uncertainties that lay ahead, he suddenly found it very pleasant to be here. This was so different from anything he'd ever known. No one had told him that new hay could smell as sweet as this, or that a rainy night could be so full of mystery. For a while he listened to the sounds around him: the beat of rain on the roof, the scurrying of mice, the faint rustling of Winkie's feet in the hay as he hunted; and once a vague, soft flapping in the rafters overhead that may have been an owl.

There had been no owl in that other barn, years ago, and no comfort save in the reassurance of Uncle Bené's arms about them...

He went rigid at the thought of Uncle Bené. "Tia!" he said urgently. "Tia—we hid in a barn like this one night, with Uncle Bené! Do—do you remember it?"

It seemed forever before she replied. Then, in a tiny whisper: "Yes. I remember. It was a big stone barn, and we hid in it the last night...before we reached the ship."

"Where did we come from?"

"I—I—please don't ask me now. But I know where we were going. We were running away, and there were men after us...men with rifles. They didn't find us till early in the morning...when we'd left the barn, and had found the little boat on the beach..."

"What happened?"

"They—they started shooting at us. We were in the little boat then, lying down on the bottom, and the fog was so thick they couldn't see us after a while. Then Uncle Bené paddled out to where the ships were, and found the one he was looking for...a Spanish ship..."

"But we weren't in Spain..."

"No, it was some other country...but the Spanish ship was the only one going to America, and he knew the captain. He paid the captain a lot of money to bring us over here..."

"And on the way over, Uncle Bené died."

"Yes." Tia's voice was so faint he could hardly hear it. "He—he was hit when the men with rifles started shooting at us, but we didn't know it till later..."

Tony had forgotten the night and the beat of rain overhead. "We're beginning to get somewhere," he said, trying to keep the excitement out of his voice. "It had to be Uncle Bené who put the money and the folder in the star box. I'll bet it was all the money he had left, and he hid it there so we'd have it later…"

"Yes," Tia whispered. "He—he didn't trust the captain, and he told us—"

Tony waited, then urged, "What did he tell us?"

"I—I don't know. Oh, Tony, don't you see? He was dying, and I'd just realized it. I was awfully little, and I couldn't talk too well, but I could understand…We'd seen some awful things…people hurt, killed…I didn't know Uncle Bené had been shot, then he told us we'd have to go on to America without him, and I saw the blood coming through his shirt." Her voice broke. "He said to pay attention to what he had to say, because it was important but to me the only important thing was that we were losing him. It gave me the most terrible feeling, and I didn't get over it till we were taken to Granny's."

"Then you don't remember what it was Uncle Bené wanted us to know?"

"Perhaps I do. I mean, I don't really forget anything, so maybe it's hidden in my head somewhere, and it'll come out when it gets ready. Please, let's talk about something pleasant."

He wanted to stay on the subject of Uncle Bené, for it seemed they were almost on the edge of learning the truth about themselves. But it would never do to force Tia. Reluctantly he began talking about the Kozaks. His mind, however, was on what had happened years ago, and he was still thinking of Uncle Bené when he fell asleep.

When he awoke suddenly, hours later, the rain had stopped and he could see a star glittering through the barn's open door. And something had entered the barn, for he was aware of slow movement and a rustling in the hay. He experienced a momentary fright, then his nostrils caught the animal scent and he saw the vague dark shapes.

"Tia," he whispered, "your friends have found us."

"I know it." She stirred and said, "They must know we're going to the mountains. I'm sure that's where they came from."

"We can't have them following us—especially to the Kozaks. Tell 'em to go away!"

"They won't hurt you."

"That's not the idea. Don't you realize that we're still in a spot? Mr. Deranian isn't going to stop looking for us after he's come this far. He's got money to spend, and he'll be paying people all around to be on the watch for us. He doesn't know about the Kozaks—but it sure won't take him long to learn if someone reports, seeing a couple bears over there."

"Oh, dear, I didn't realize…How long is it till daylight?"

"Couple hours. If these crazy bears will just stay here and sleep, I wouldn't mind starting for the Kozaks now."

"Let's try it."

They got their bags and crept from the barn.

It was hard going at first, for the pasture ended directly behind the barn and they were forced to climb a long wooded slope in the dark. Soon they stumbled upon what seemed to be a cattle trail, and after much winding they came out suddenly upon a bare hilltop.

Tony looked around him in amazement. It was a clear, moonless night, and from where he stood he could see—and for the first time in his life—the full sweep of the heavens. In the city he had never noticed the stars; usually they were hidden behind smog or overcast, and even on the few clear nights the crowding buildings shut out the view. And Heron Lake had always been cloudy.

Now he stood, incredulous, before the glittering display overhead. Tia seized his arm suddenly and pointed, and he turned and saw his first shooting star. The sight brought a curious prickling to his neck.

He said in wonderment, "There must be spaceships out there somewhere, and other people…"

"I'm sure of it," said Tia. Then, "Tony, why did you tell that policeman at the bus station that our name was Castaway?"

"I—I don't know. It just popped out. Maybe it was because I'd been trying to think of something between Caroway and Hideaway. Why?"

It was a long time before she answered. Finally she whispered slowly, "*Castaway*," and her hand swept the sky. "I think we *are* Castaways—and that we came from out there somewhere."

"Now that doesn't make sense."

"Does *everything* have to make sense? People would say that *we* didn't make sense, just because we're not like everybody else. We had to come from *somewhere*—and if you can believe there are other people out there, why is it so hard to believe that we might have come from where *they* are?"

"O.K. But we won't know the truth till we get to Stony Creek, and we've got to find Kozak's first. Which way is north?"

Neither knew the North Star by sight, but Tia was able to find it by first locating the Dipper, which she had no trouble remembering from star charts she had seen. Even with his directions straightened out, Tony had only a vague idea where they were, but he reasoned they could reach the Kozak orchard by heading straight west. If they missed the orchard itself, at least they ought to come out on the road that led to it, which was north of Red Bank.

Their progress was still painfully slow, but presently it became easier as the sky lightened. Now the black mass of the mountains ahead became clearer in outline, and suddenly the higher peaks and ridges were edged with the first crimson light of dawn. They stopped for a while, enthralled, watching the color creep slowly down the slopes as the sleepy world around them began to awake. Finally they trudged on, following cow paths and country lanes when they could, then cutting straight across the fields in order to get back on course.

The rising sun was topping the hills behind them when Tony glanced back and saw the bears.

"Oh, no!" he groaned. "Tell 'em to go away, Tia."

It was soon apparent that the bears had no intention of leaving them. Whenever Tia scolded them, they would look at her wistfully as if to say: "You are our friends, and you're going in the same direction we are, so why can't we all travel together?"

Because his attention was on the bears, he almost walked into a farmyard before he saw it.

He was taking his time carrying Winkie when it happened, and they were going downhill, following a path along a strip of woods. The little cat suddenly leaped away. Too late Tony saw the weatherbeaten shack on the left, where the woods ended. He was instantly aware of the man in faded overalls who sat on the back steps, for the man was staring up at him, slack-jawed, as if it were impossible to believe the sight of two human beings and two black bears, who seemed about to enter the yard.

Abruptly the man leaped up and sprang into the house. Tony heard him say hoarsely, "Hand me the gun! *It's them witch people— bears an' all!*"

Tony caught Tia's hand and jerked her into the cover of the woods. As they ran, a shotgun blast sent bits of leaves falling in the green twilight ahead. They dodged behind a large tree and scrambled on through the shadows as another blast sounded behind them.

Long minutes later, after splashing across a rocky stream, they reached the far edge of the woods and fell, panting, in a bed of ferns that grew along the top of an embankment. Below them, following a much larger stream, was a narrow gravel road that wound away through a valley. At the moment, going any farther was unthinkable, for they could hear traffic on the road and see farmhouses beyond a bridge downstream.

When she had got her breath, Tia turned stricken eyes to him and said, "I—I don't understand. That man called us *witch people!* And why would he *shoot* at us?"

Tony looked grimly at the road, and a little longingly at the creek, and wished they'd stopped to drink at the stream they'd crossed. He was very thirsty.

"It was seeing us with the bears," he muttered. "He must have heard about us over the radio, and realized who we were. It scared him."

"But—but why?"

"You oughta know we can't go hiking around the country with wild animals without giving some people the shakes. And didn't you hear what Ben Purdy called us?"

Then he shook his head. "I guess you didn't. You were busy at the bear cage. Anyway, after what we did at that police station, he was really scared. Said we couldn't be human—that we must be witches."

"Oh, dear!"

He was trying to get his direction straightened out when two cars came by, moving slowly. Then came a third car, barely creeping along. The driver was speaking over a two-way radio, and though the conversation was muffled, their sharp ears could distinguish every word of it.

"...We're up on Yellow Creek Road," the driver was saying.

"About two miles from the highway, near Mace Johnson's place. Got it straight?"

"We got it," came the reply. "What about the bears?"

"Mace says he seen 'em crossing the creek just a couple minutes ago. We figger those witch people can't be too far off—mebbe up here in the timber above the creek. There ain't but six of us up this way, so we're gonna need some help. You guys get over here fast!"

"Coming!"

A cold knot was clutching in Tony's stomach. It seemed, suddenly, that every man's hand was turned against them.

He looked bleakly at Tia, and whispered, "Let's get away from here."

APPLE ORCHARD

They crawled back until they were well out of sight of the road, then began hurrying through the woods in an upstream direction. The bears, Tony reasoned, must have crossed the creek somewhere near the bridge, and he wanted to get as far from there as possible before slipping out of the woods.

Several times in the next few minutes they heard cars moving slowly along the road, patrolling from both directions, but gradually these sounds faded as the narrowing valley swung to the left, curving past a jutting ridge. Tony moved straight on, climbing steadily until they were over the ridge, and then angling cautiously down through a cutover area on the other side. Reaching the safety of a thicket of young pines, they stopped to get their bearings, for just ahead was another road, and beyond that lay a farm. The farm sprawled over a hill, and directly behind it rose a mountain.

Tony ran his tongue over dry lips and forgot his thirst. "Kozak's can't be far from here," he said, looking wonderingly at the cool heights ahead. "The way I figure it, that road runs sort of west. Maybe it runs into the one we want. What's the name of it?"

"Cahill Road, and the Kozaks live four miles north on it." Tia rubbed a grimy hand over her smudged face. "Oh, dear," she added. "The Kozaks must have heard all about us by now. What if they don't want anything to do with us?"

Tony experienced a momentary jolt at the thought of being hunted and having no haven to run to. But instantly he shook his head. "Don't talk that way. If they're Father O'Day's friends, you know they'll have more sense than these other people. Let's get going."

"Wait—where's Winkie?"

"I haven't seen him since we were shot at. Don't worry about him. He always manages to catch up with us."

During the rest of the morning there was no sign of Winkie—or the bears either, for which he was thankful. Ever on the alert for people, they followed the road a while, taking cover in the shrubbery when they heard cars approaching; later, when the road turned in the wrong direction, they skirted a farm and began angling over the rising hills.

Once, after they had stopped to drink from a trickle of water coming from a ledge, he closed his eyes and tried to visualize the Kozak place. He saw, clearly, a long hill entirely covered with a grove; on one side, nearly hidden by the trees, was a large red brick house. A paved road ran in front of it.

When they reached the crest of the rocky hill they had been climbing, he looked hopefully ahead and glimpsed a paved road in the distance.

"There it is," he said, pointing. "You can just make out the orchard."

"I hope it's the right place," Tia said wearily. "I—I can't go much farther…"

Her pinched face told him how tired she was. He realized with a shock that they had been traveling for nearly eleven hours since they left the barn, and in all that time they'd had nothing to eat. Nor had they eaten very much yesterday.

"We'll be there in thirty minutes," he assured her.

Before they went down the slope she looked worriedly back over the way they had come. Her voice broke as she said, "Oh Winkie, where *are* you? Do you suppose he's *hurt,* Tony?"

"I told you he's all right. He jumped away before that man shot, and you know he can't walk as fast as we can. And cats don't hurry for anybody."

Instead of the half hour he had promised her, it took them more than double that time to circle through woods and around fields to the lower corner of the orchard. In his eagerness to reach the house and be among friendly people, he almost forgot his tired feet, and it was with difficulty that he restrained himself and approached the place warily.

"They may have visitors," he whispered, between bites of an apple he had plucked. "We'd better scout things out before we show ourselves."

They crept down through the rows of heavily laden trees, and paused uncertainly near a group of neat outbuildings. In the noonday stillness they could hear no sound save distant cars somewhere on the road. Frowning, Tony led the way on, to a large open shed on one side of a parking area. Just beyond it lay the house—the big brick building he'd visioned earlier.

Tia clutched his arm. "There—there's no one here," she whispered.

"But there *must* be! Father O'Day phoned them—they know we were coming."

Could he have made a mistake and come to the wrong place? But no, that couldn't be. In neat stacks beside him under the shed were hundreds of new crates. On each crate was stenciled KOZAK ORCHARDS.

Tia's chin began to tremble. "I—I didn't want to tell you, but I've had the awfullest feeling for hours…"

He stared around in sick dismay, noting the closed windows and drawn curtains, and the blown leaves and debris on the side porch. From the looks of things, no one had been here for a week. The Kozaks must have gone away somewhat before Father O'Day telephoned them.

Tia sank helplessly upon a crate and put her hands over her face. Tony rubbed grimy knuckles across his jaw, and his lips thinned. They'd come hundreds of miles to find the one person who could help them—and now this.

What were they going to do?

"If we've come this far by ourselves, we can make it the rest of the way," Tony ground out.

Suddenly he was aware that one of the cars he had heard on the road was now very close and slowing. He glanced down the long driveway, and saw it turning in at the entrance. With a quick rise of hope he wondered if it could be the Kozaks returning. Then caution told he couldn't take that chance. There were too many witch-hunters on the roads.

Tia was already on her feet, looking anxiously around for a place to hide. But beyond the open shed there was no spot near enough to reach without being seen.

"Get behind the crates," said Tony. "Quick!"

They caught up their bags and crouched down behind a stack of crates, and hurriedly rearranged some of the other stacks around them. Between the crates they watched a white sedan roll quietly to a stop in the middle of the parking area.

Almost in slow motion, two men got out and stood poised in watchful silence on either side of the car. The slender and rather grim man in brown was Lucas Deranian. Today he looked more than ever like Father O'Day's archenemy, the devil.

* * *

After the trouble they had had, the shock of seeing Mr. Deranian was almost too much. How, Tony wondered incredulously, had the man ever discovered that Tia and he were coming here? It seemed impossible.

The other man, a pale and much heavier person in a rumpled gray suit, must be the one Tia had seen at the door of the mission. There was a look about him that Tony had always associated with detectives. Was he the Werner Karman who had called Ben Purdy from Washington?

The two men spoke in tones so low that ordinary ears could not have heard them.

Tight-lipped, the pale man said, "What do you think, Lucas?"

"Don't know yet. They could be here now—probably hiding in the house. If locks can't hold them…"

The pale man's eyes roved restlessly, taking in the shed, the outbuildings, and the closed windows of the house. His lips barely moved as he said, "When I asked about the Kozaks, I was told they'd been away for a week. You really think that priest would send those kids here, not knowing his friends were gone?"

"That has to be the answer. We were crowding him close the other morning. If we'd just found out earlier that he knew these people…Werner, you'd better search the house. Think you can get in?"

"I ought to have a master key that will make it. Keep your eye on the side door. I'll go in the front way."

The man in brown nodded. "Watch it, Werner—you know what we're up against."

The other said softly, "That's just it—I *don't* know."

"You know as much as the rest of us. We were warned to expect anything."

"Yeah. But I wouldn't have dreamed…"

The pale man—he had to be Werner Karman—took a heavy bunch of keys from his pocket and moved quietly around to the front of the house. Lucas Deranian stood motionless by the car watching and listening. The minutes dragged by.

Finally the pale man returned, shaking his head. "No one's been in there for days, Lucas."

"You checked the kitchen carefully?"

The other nodded. "And the cellar. No food has been touched."

Lucas Deranian smiled grimly. "Then there's a possibility we got here ahead of them."

"Maybe. But hold it a little longer. I'd better have a look at these other buildings."

Tony chilled, and he felt Tia's small hand tremble on his arm. The pale man was striding straight toward them, his restless eyes roving over the stacks of crates. But the man paused only briefly and hurried on to the closed garage and storage buildings beyond.

Werner Karman was gone longer this time. When he came back he was almost running. "They're here somewhere," he whispered tensely. "I found two apple cores back there. Fresh ones. The juice is still wet on them."

"See any tracks?"

"Not in this gravel. And there's too much grass around the trees. They're not in the outbuildings—I checked them all first. They probably saw us coming and ran back into the orchard."

"Now wait a moment. Some farm children around here could have been stealing apples."

"I doubt it. I was raised in apple country. These won't be ready to pick till next month—but you can always find a few early ripe ones. Nobody would eat green ones, right down to the core, unless he was very hungry and didn't know how to find ripe ones." The pale man shook his head. "I was beginning to think that priest may have had some other friends over by Fairview, and that the kids had really gone there. But this proves they didn't."

He paused, and muttered, "How are we going to handle this?"

The grim man in brown began snapping his fingers. "Let me think. Somehow I don't like the idea of playing hide-and-seek in a big orchard…"

"What else can we do? Don't forget—there are six of us. I could go and tell the others to spread out—"

"No, Werner. Too risky."

"Why?"

"You know why! With this country full of witch hunters? That fool Purdy! He's got the whole area seething. If those kids got away from us and someone spotted them—or anyone on the road saw us hunting them—there'd be a mob here in no time."

"Maybe you're right. This witch business has sure gotten out of hand. But how are we going to manage it? We can't afford to lose those kids. Not now. They've already upset the whole schedule…"

"Forget the schedule. Ships can be delayed." Mr. Deranian shrugged. "As for our connections abroad—if they'd told me ten years ago what they'd lost, I could have returned their prizes immediately. But they were so secretive…" He shrugged again. "How could anyone have even dreamed that those refugee kids I left with the old woman…"

"Lucas, what are we going to do? We haven't got all day."

"Yes, we have—what there is left of it."

"Eh? What's your idea?"

"It's quite simple. We'll just drive off for a while and give them a chance to enter the house."

"Huh?"

"Werner, unless that pair can fly—and I wouldn't be surprised to discover they can—they must have hiked nearly twenty miles today. Except for some green apples, I doubt if they've had anything to eat since they got off the bus yesterday. Purdy didn't feed them. So they are tired now, and very hungry. This is their destination, and they'll be forced to use it. Do you see my point?"

The pale man grunted. "I get you. They'll be in that house the minute we're gone, looking for something to eat. In another hour they'll be asleep. Then we can slip up to the house, surround it, and take them easily."

"Of course. Now let's get back where the others are waiting."

"Hold it. Someone's coming."

Lucas Deranian turned.

In their hiding place behind the crates Tony looked at Tia's pinched face, and clenched his fists in growing desperation. He had, in fact, been planning to enter the house as soon as the men left, not only to find food, but to outfit themselves for the rest of the journey. It was not a thing he cared to do, but how could they possibly manage otherwise? They *had* to have food—and they'd also need blankets, matches, a knife, and a map if he could find one. He'd leave a note for Mr. Kozak, and plenty of money to pay for the things they took. But now…

He watched a small car come up the driveway and stop behind the other one. Two eager young men in sport shirts got out. One, who carried a notebook, said quickly, "We're trying to find Mr. Werner Karman. Are you Mr. Karman, sir?"

The pale man's face lost expression. "What made you come looking for him over here?"

"Why, sir, we—we had your description, and we traced you from Fairview to Red Bank, and a boy at a filling station said some men in a car like yours were asking about the Kozak place. You *are* Mr. Karman, aren't you?"

"What do you want?"

"A statement, sir. We're from the Press. We have statements from all the witnesses who saw what happened yesterday at Fairview; now we need one from you. What happened is absolutely incredible—but it happened, and you're the only person who can give us any answers."

"No comment," Werner Karman said coldly.

"Oh, come on!" the other young man burst out. "This is the story of the year! There are reporters from some of the big papers looking all over for you; they're bound to find you soon. We're just local correspondents—so please give us a break. Why did you come to the Kozak place? Do you expect to find those witch kids over here?"

Mr. Deranian said quickly, "It happens that Mr. Kozak is an old friend of mine. He knows the country here, and we were hoping he could give us some help. Unfortunately, he's still away from home. Now if you'll excuse us, gentlemen, we must be going. This is an urgent matter, and we're not at liberty to discuss it."

"But won't you give us a few clues?" begged the young man with the notebook. "They are not really kids, are they? Could they actually be witches? Or would you say they're something in human form from outer space? It's being said the Government captured them, and was holding them—I mean, *trying* to hold them—for study when they escaped. Is that true?"

"No comment," said Werner Karman again. "Now please—"

"Just a moment, sir. Did you know they were shot at this morning? A farmer named Hogan over on Yellow Creek Road shot at them twice, at close range. He told us that if they'd been real human beings—"

"Did he hit them?" Mr. Deranian interrupted.

"He couldn't, and he's known to be a marksman. Hogan swears he saw the shot glance away as if he'd struck an invisible wall. There's no mistake about it, because those creatures were traveling with the bears when it happened, and Hogan's wife and brother both saw the whole thing."

"What we'd like to know," the other young man put in hastily, "is how dangerous they are. If they *are* dangerous, we think the public should be warned."

"Sorry," said Mr. Deranian, "but this is a Government matter. We are not allowed to discuss it. Our advice—and let it be a warning—is for everyone to leave them strictly alone, and give us a chance to do our duty."

"But if you caught them, how would you hold them? If they can go through locked doors—"

"There are ways."

Werner Karman said, "We've no more time for questions. Let's get moving, Lucas." He slid into the car beside Mr. Deranian, and ignoring the protests of the two young men, drove around the smaller car and headed down the driveway.

The young man with the notebook said, "Let's give them a couple minutes, Bill, then follow them."

"Guess we'd better. That's the only way we'll learn anything. Say, how *would* you hold a couple fugitives like that crazy pair, if they can open any lock?"

"Dunno, unless you doped them and put them to sleep. Say, do you see what I see?"

The two men were suddenly staring in the direction of the outbuildings.

"Good grief!" one whispered. "Those are Ben Purdy's bears!"

"Yeah—and you know what that means. We'd better catch Karman and tell him to get back here."

Tony swallowed and glanced at Tia, huddled in silent misery beside him. As the two young men leaped into their car, he closed his eyes and prayed for a miracle.

WITCH TRAP

It seemed to Tony that he had hardly finished his prayer before it was answered. As he opened his eyes he glimpsed the small car rushing down the drive. At this moment, distinctly, he heard his name whispered from some point beyond the far corner of the house.

"Tony?" came the whisper. "Tony? If you can hear me, *don't* reply—other ears are listening. Just send me a sign. This is Father O'Day." A moment's pause, then urgently, "Hurry—there isn't much time!"

Tony trembled with sudden excitement and relief. Suppressing a desire to leap shouting to his feet, he drew out his harmonica and blew softly into it. A large white pebble bounced across the parking area, took off, sailed past the house in the direction of the whisper, and tapped lightly upon the stones of an outdoor fireplace before it dropped.

"Praise be!" the whisper came again, fervently. "Tony, if you are hiding among those crates, give me two taps."

The pebble rose again and struck twice upon the fireplace. "Good! Now, Tony, you two start crawling out of the back of the shed—then keep crawling till you can see the road. If I'm not there waiting, hide till I drive by. I have to leave now—someone's coming."

Tony hesitated a moment, wondering if Father O'Day realized all that had been going on here. He doubted it, for the priest seemed to be too far away for his only normal ears to have heard everything that had been said. Nor was there any way to tell him now without being overheard by someone else.

Tia had already thrust some of the crates aside and was backing out of their hiding place. He followed, and they crawled stealthily from the rear of the shed and began snaking down through the tall grass of the orchard, angling for the road. Momentarily he expected to see the bears come ambling behind them like a pair of happy black clowns. But there was still no sign of them when they reached the edge of the orchard, long minutes later. Nor was Father O'Day anywhere in evidence on the road.

An old truck clattered by, followed presently by a farm tractor and a slowly moving station wagon. The station wagon was crowded with men, and most of them seemed to be carrying guns. They had to be witch hunters.

A finger of coldness crept down Tony's spine. Was the hunt spreading out to the mountains, or had someone told them that the bears had been seen near here?

The station wagon did not stop, but his relief was only temporary. The hunt was spreading out. Soon, when it was learned that the bears were here, the orchard would be swarming with hunters.

What had happened to Father O'Day?

Suddenly, from some point beyond the lower side of the orchard, he heard a car start up and move toward the road. With his acute sense of hearing he could almost judge its location and speed, and he was aware that it was barely creeping along in low gear. After a while it stopped, as if the driver were studying the way ahead; abruptly, with a clash of gears, it whirled into the road and approached with the motor racing.

It was an old car, so spattered with mud that it was almost unrecognizable at first sight. Not until it was a hundred yards away, and slowing, could Tony make out the big figure at the wheel. The driver was wearing faded khakis, sunglasses, and a battered tourist cap, and he might have been some camper or fisherman on his way into the mountains.

For a moment, with the sun glinting across the windshield, Tony was uncertain. But Tia leaped up without hesitation, and said happily, "That's Father O'Day! Hurry—I can hear more cars coming!" They raced for the road and scrambled into the back of the car as it stopped briefly for them.

"Thanks be to Heaven!" the priest said feelingly, and sent the car rushing ahead again. "Get down on the floor and pull that tarpaulin over you."

As Tony raised the tarpaulin, something soft and black brushed against him and he heard a familiar meow of greeting. Tia gave a delighted cry that was actually audible. She hugged Father O'Day, then slid under the tarpaulin with Winkie clasped in her arms.

"How in the world did you happen to find Winkie?" Tony asked in amazement.

"I didn't find him," the big man rumbled. "He found me. About an hour ago. I'd been watching for you all morning, and I'd about decided I'd better start searching along some of the back roads when the little rascal appeared. If he hadn't come when he did…" There was a pause, then the priest added, "I'm sorry I let you two in for so much trouble, but it couldn't be helped. Of all the incredible…"

"I don't see how anything could have been helped," Tony said. "Who was it listening back there in the orchard when you first called to us?"

"Augie Kozak's hired man, an old fellow named Sam Meeks. Sam's a good soul, bless him, but we couldn't chance having him recognize me. Not with the way things are. Ah, the shock I had when

I found I'd sent you on a long journey to an empty house! When I couldn't get Augie on the phone, I called old Sam, and discovered Augie and his family had gone to Canada for the month. I almost told Sam to meet you at the bus, and decided I'd better not."

"Why not?"

"Oh, Sam's a bit simple. He would have talked. And I realized that a man as clever as Deranian was going to trace you, in spite of precautions. So I decided I'd better get down here myself, as fast as I could."

Tony swallowed. "We sure are glad to see you! But honest, we're awfully sorry about things. We've caused you such a lot of trouble—"

"Nonsense! Fighting trouble is half my existence. Tried to get here in time to meet the bus—not that it would have done any good—but I was delayed. Had to get a substitute at the Mission, and make other arrangements in a hurry. On the way down I had to stop and have the car worked on—the clutch was going bad. Then I heard the news. Of all things to happen! It's in every paper I've seen, and on the radio."

Father O'Day paused. "Odd, but it was the bears that really shook people. Sort of clinched the witch idea in the public mind. Tia, did you *have* to open that cage?"

Tony was aware that they were swinging around curves and gradually climbing. He said, "Father, she *had* to do it—you ought to see those poor bears. They were half starved, and there wasn't even any water in their cage."

"I saw them—got just a glimpse when I was crawling back to where I'd hidden the car. Tia, I don't blame you for freeing them—I hate to see wild animals locked in cages. But two black bears, plus a black cat and a whirling broom, are a heavy dose for some people. This country's gone quite out of its mind—"

The big man stopped abruptly. He grunted. "Saints preserve us!" he growled. "Looks as if we're running into a roadblock. We can't turn—back they've seen us. They're guarding the river bridge—it's the only way into the mountains from here. Hurry—get down under that camping equipment, and don't move. Hang on to Winkie, and may Heaven protect all stray black cats…"

Tony quickly shifted some blankets and burrowed under them with Tia. As he drew the corner of the tarpaulin down tight, he felt the car moving. It stopped, and now he could make out low voices and the scuffling of many feet.

Father O'Day's deep voice rang out cheerfully, "Hello, every-body! What seems to be wrong?"

Stark silence greeted him. Finally someone muttered, "If you don't know what's wrong, mister, you better git your head looked after. Or don't you read the papers?"

An older voice said, "Lay off him, Joe. Can't you see he's just another tourist on a camping trip? What we aim to know, mister, is have you seen them witch people sneaking around—or maybe them bears they're traveling with? An' don't tell me you ain't heard the news—everybody knows about 'em now!"

"Oh, I've heard about them," the big man said easily. "But I can hardly believe they're witches."

"We don't care what you believe, stranger," a third voice said harshly. "But when a foxy-faced thing that looks like a girl goes up to a bear cage, one that's locked with two big rusted padlocks you couldn't budge with anything less'n a blowtorch, an' jerks 'em open like they was made of butter, then I say she's either a witch or something worse. Ten, twelve, people seen her do it. An' I reckon everybody around here has seen what the boy varmint done to the inside of the Fairview police station. He just stood there an' blowed on his harmonica a little bit, an' that place near tore itself apart. Them's facts, stranger. An' you can't go against facts."

"Extraordinary," Father O'Day said. "Most extraordinary. But why are you all waiting—"

He was interrupted by a blare of static from a shortwave radio, followed by an excited announcement: "*Attention, all searchers! Attention! The bears were seen at Kozak Orchards less than an hour ago! I repeat, the bears were seen at Kozak Orchards...*"

The volume was turned down, and the man who had spoken last exclaimed, "I told you so! They're coming this way. They're headin' straight for Witch Mountain!"

"Witch Mountain?" Father O'Day repeated.

"That's right. Witch Mountain. To git there you gotta cross this bridge." The harsh voice rose. "All right, boys, before you scatter out an' take your places, make up your minds! You aiming to blast 'em, or take 'em alive?"

Immediately a half dozen voices began to argue.

"You can't take 'em alive!"

"Ben Purdy, he took 'em!"

"That's right, Ben took 'em—he just didn't know how to hang on to 'em."

"I tell you, you *can't* take 'em alive! The only reason Ben Purdy done it was because there was folks around, an' they didn't want to give theirselves away. But now that everybody knows what they are—"

"Aw, shaddup! You ain't talkin' sense. I say blast 'em. That's the *only* way—"

"Blast 'em with what? You got any silver bullet? Didn't you hear what happened this morning over on Yellow Creek? Feller aimed right *at* 'em—an' never even touched 'em!"

"Now listen to me, fellers: you know the Government wants them critters back. I hear they're offering a big reward—"

Father O'Day's deep voice drowned out the others, "Just a moment, gentlemen! As long as you have loaded guns, do you realize the danger every child around here is in? Suppose, in your desire to kill a witch, you made a terrible mistake and killed one of your neighbor's children. How would you feel? How would *he* feel?"

No one answered. In the silence that followed, Tony could hear the heavy breathing of the men around the car, and the uneasy shuffling of their feet.

"One more thing," the deep voice of the priest went on. "If these witches haven't harmed you, why try to harm them? Why not let them go where they're going? If you're *sure* they're headed for Witch Mountain…"

He paused, and the man with the harsh voice said, "'Course we're sure! Where else would they go? That's witch country. Everybody knows about it."

"Seems I've heard about it," Father O'Day admitted. "How long have they been there?"

"First of 'em come to Witch Mountain way back in my gran'daddy's day."

"And they're still there?"

"They come an' go, seems like. It's said they left for a long spell, but that some came back about ten, twelve, years ago. Leastways, that's when the music started up again, an' the lights. For a little while."

"Music? Lights?"

"That's what I said, stranger!" The man was becoming irritated by the questioning. "How come you're so powerful curious about Witch Mountain?"

"You make me curious."

"Well, if you got any fool notions about going there, you better git over 'em right away. Ain't no proper road to Witch Mountain, an' the only folks what live near there are them dumb summer people—an' they ain't got no better sense."

"Thank you," said the priest, and now his voice was unusually soft. "Witch Mountain. Yes, I'm beginning to remember about it. If I recall correctly, it's over near a little place named—isn't it Stony Creek?"

"You go through Stony Creek. But you got to go way on over the gap to Misty Valley. It's near there."

"Oh. Misty Valley." Father O'Day's voice sounded doubtful. "Well, thank you again. If you good gentlemen will let me over the bridge, I'll be on my way."

As the car clattered across the bridge, Tony lay clenching his hands in alternate hope, uncertainty, and despair. Tia whispered, "It's all become so—so *confusing*. What do you think about it, Tony?"

"I don't know what to think. That witch business got me going at first. But it's been so many years…"

"Tony, what will we *do* if there's no one left?"

"We'll make out. Tia, don't you *feel* anything about it? You nearly always have *some* sort of feelings about things…"

"Not now. I—I'm just too tired and hungry…"

Father O'Day said, "You two can come up for air. But keep your heads down, and be ready to pull that tarpaulin over you. We won't be out of danger till we get where we're going."

"Are—are we going to Stony Creek?" Tony asked hesitantly. "Or Misty Valley?"

"It's too late to go to either place. And much too risky at the moment. I spattered mud over the car so Augie's hired man wouldn't recognize it, but if he happened to see the license plate...Anyway, we've got a lot to talk over, and I'm hoping Tia's memory will help us. Has she thought of anything new?"

"Yes, sir. A lot."

"Good! As soon as we make camp we'll have a powwow. Wish I could take you to a motel so you could clean up and get a full night's rest—but that's out. We've got to hide. Have you two ever been camping?"

"We sort of camped at Heron Lake."

"That's not the real thing. Before I left the Mission I had a hunch we might be forced to play hide-and-seek. So I tossed in plenty of blankets and all my old camping equipment. Then, when I read the news about you, I realized I'd better do some disguising. It won't fool Deranian if he gets a close look at me—but let's hope he doesn't look twice. At a glance I'm only another camper in a dirty car. Of course, he must realize that I would surely come down to hunt you—but we'll talk about that later."

Suddenly he grunted, and asked slowly, "When was the last time you two had a decent meal?"

"I guess it was early yesterday morning."

"Ump! That's a long stretch. And there are no hamburger stands in this direction. If you can hold out for another hour, I'll cook you up a real camp dinner."

Tony twisted about in the narrow space until he and Tia had made themselves fairly comfortable. Winkie, curled on a blanket between them, began purring contentedly.

The sound of the tires changed as they turned into a gravel road. The motor labored as they began to climb. Tony realized they must be well into the mountains. He was wondering if it would be safe to raise the tarpaulin and glance out, when all at once there came to him a clear recollection of Uncle Bené.

It was only a flash, followed by other flashes that seemed to have no connection: Uncle Bené speaking to them, taking them from a place where they'd been imprisoned; and a sudden frightening memory of an accident or a wreck—was it a smashed lifeboat?...

"Tia!" he said. "Tia, I've just remembered some things! Weren't we in a lifeboat—one that was wrecked?"

"Yes," she whispered. "But don't ask me about it now."

"Tia, this is important!"

"I know it, but Stony Creek is more important. It was one of the things Uncle Bené told us not to forget. If I were not so tired, I think I could remember it all..."

"He must have told us to go there, because it was marked on the map."

"Yes, he did..." Her voice sounded very weary.

"He told us to go there and—and meet someone."

"Who?"

"Someone named—Castaway."

CAMP

It was nearly twilight when Father O'Day stopped the car, announced that all was safe, and the two passengers crawled stiffly from their hiding place.

Tony hardly knew what to expect. A few minutes earlier the car had turned from the gravel road and gone winding and bumping upward on a grade that had seemed almost too much for it. Now he peered about wordlessly, drinking in sights and sounds and smells he had never dreamed of experiencing.

They seemed to be high up in a glade of crowding evergreens. The air was cold and sweet with a forest fragrance, and alive with birdsong and the chuckle and gurgle of water running over rocks. Turning, he saw a small brook that came down out of the shadows in a series of crystal pools. In the deep blue of the valley far below he was aware of the wild rush of a larger stream. As he raised his eyes to a break in the foliage, he gasped at the sight of a great forested mountain slowly vanishing in a veil of mist.

"Like it?" said Father O'Day, lifting a frying pan and a coffeepot from the trunk of the car.

Tia nodded, and Tony said, "It's great! Where—where are we?"

"You might call it the backyard of an old fellow I know. He lives on the other side of the mountain, but I have permission to camp here whenever I wish."

The priest drew soap and towels from the trunk. "Take your pick of the pools, and get yourselves cleaned up. By the time you're through, dinner will be ready."

"B-but don't you need our help?"

"Not this evening. You've been on the run for three days. You'll be surprised how much better a bath and a change of clothes will make you feel."

Tony, after he had chosen his pool and stripped off his dirty clothing, was astounded at the icy coldness of the water. Presently, after he had rubbed down and changed to a clean shirt and jeans from his bag, his shivering stopped. Now, as he smelled the woodsmoke, he was suddenly aware of the overpowering aroma of food being cooked over a campfire.

It was corned beef hash, enough of it to have served twice their number. Before they ate, Father O'Day gave a heartfelt prayer.

"Heavenly Father," the big man began, "we thank you for giving us sanctuary for the night. Please forgive the foolish, the ignorant, and the greedy who have beset us, and help us to solve the tangled problem that has brought us so far. Amen."

It was black dark when they finished eating, and the fire had died to a glowing mass of coals. The priest tossed a few sticks upon the embers, and in the light of their burning the pans were cleaned, and tarpaulins, camp mattresses, and blankets were spread around the fire.

"Before we have our powwow," the priest said, "I think we'd better rest a bit. Frankly, it's been quite a day."

Tony, wearily drawing a blanket about him, was asleep before his head touched the mattress.

When he awoke, hours later, the clock he instantly visualized told him that it was after three in the morning. It was about the same time, he remembered, that he had wakened in the barn when the bears came. Was it only yesterday? So much had happened that it seemed like days and days had gone by...

Suddenly he remembered Uncle Bené. He raised up and glanced quickly over at Tia, hoping she was awake. By the vague light of the stars that came through the break in the foliage, he could make out her huddled form. She was still asleep, apparently clutching Winkie, for he could hear a soft purring coming from the blanket. In spite of his eagerness to find out all about Uncle Bené, he did not have the heart to disturb her.

As he realized by the steady breathing on the other side of him that Father O'Day was also asleep, Tony's mind turned to Witch Mountain. Earlier, on the way to camp, he'd visualized the place, but had seen only another sprawling mountain, half shrouded in mist, rising above a deep gorge where a stream ran white over boulders. Now, hopefully, he managed to picture it again, but not the faintest light broke its expanse of darkness. It did look sort of haunted, though.

Haunted? No, he told himself, the place wasn't haunted, and there were no such things as witches. Unless—and the skin on his neck prickled at the thought—he and Tia really did belong to the witch tribe. But that couldn't be true. And he'd better forget the story he'd overheard at the bridge. It was just a lot of superstitious bunk, the sort of thing that ignorant people were always imagining. Probably there never had been anyone living on Witch Mountain, and if he had any sense he'd put the whole thing out of his mind.

Only, there'd been that part about the witches returning—at about the time he and Tia were trying to escape and come here with Uncle Bené. And there was that mention of lights and music. *Music?*...

Unconsciously Tony reached for his harmonica and raised it to his lips. As he breathed softly into it, and a little sadly, he wondered what kind of music his people would have played—if there *had* been music on the mountain, and if it had been *his* people who had played it. Probably it would have been forest music—the kind he could hear all about him now in the chirp of crickets, the song of the brook, and the mysterious little movements of unknown forest creatures that he was aware of all about him.

The melody that began to flow from his harmonica blended with the brook's song and the whisper of the night wind. Leaves played tag overhead, and two rabbits ventured into the starlit glade. They were followed by another and another; as the music continued, still larger listeners appeared—several does with fawns who ringed the glade, enthralled by this curious and lovely magic of the night.

Then abruptly the spell was broken by a very human cough. In a flash all the listening creatures vanished in the shadows. Grumbling, Father O'Day sat up.

"Forgive me for being a dolt! Ah, Tony, I held that cough back as long as I could. You may not be a witch, my boy, but that was pure witchery you were creating. Did you see all the deer?"

"Yes, sir." They were the first wild ones he'd ever seen, and ordinarily he might have been amazed by the sight. But somehow, here in this seclusion of the forest, it seemed perfectly natural. All at once he knew that, no matter what happened, he and Tia could never go back and live in the city.

Tia, he saw, was also awake and sitting up. She said, "Did you see the littlest fawn, Tony? It was the cutest thing! Oh, I hope we have *lots* of animals where we're going."

Tony managed not to laugh. The way animals took up with Tia, she'd probably need a whole mountain to herself. "We don't know where we're going yet," he said. "Let's hear the rest about Uncle Bené."

"Just a moment," said Father O'Day. "Before you get too far ahead of me, give me a chance to catch up. Tony, who was Uncle Bené?"

"He was the man who was bringing us to America. Tia remembered him first. That got me started, and I've been remembering more about him ever since..."

Tony closed his eyes, and said, "He was a small, quick man with a beard—not a relative, but he was one of us, and we loved him. We'd been caught in a lot of trouble—soldiers were everywhere—and we were trying to escape and reach the sea." He glanced at the dark bulk of Father O'Day in the shadow beyond him, and asked, "Do you remember about any trouble in Europe at that time?"

"Yes," the big man said. "There was a rebellion in Hungary against the communists, and for a long time afterward there was scattered trouble here and there."

"Well, all I can remember about it now is that Tia and I were prisoners, and were kept in an old house with a high wall around it. We hadn't seen Uncle Bené for weeks and weeks, not since the accident—"

"Accident?" the priest said quietly.

"Yes. Tia will have to explain about that. It's coming back to me—that there *was* an accident, and our lifeboat was smashed. Is that right, Tia?"

"Yes," she whispered, as if it hurt her to speak.

"It seems that Tia, Uncle Bené, and myself were the only ones who were not hurt or killed. Then the soldiers came and captured us all." Tony paused, and said, "Why would they treat people that way?"

"Because human rights and human suffering mean nothing to a communist," the big man growled. "Only the state is important to them."

"Oh, I see. Well, Uncle Bené managed to get away. He was like Tia—no lock could hold him. And of course Tia was too small to open locks at that time. Anyway, when the fighting started, Uncle Bené came and took us out of the house where we were, and escaped with us. We spent days running and hiding until we reached the coast. It seems that Uncle Bené had had time to plan how to get us away—he'd written over here for money, and he'd made a deal with the captain of a Spanish ship. He didn't trust the man, but it was our only chance…"

Tony paused, unconsciously clenching his hands as he recalled the terror and heartbreak of that experience. Then he hastened on, telling of their last night ashore in the stone barn, of slipping down to the beach in the dawn, and of getting away in the little boat just as the soldiers discovered them and began to fire.

"We didn't know Uncle Bené had been hit. He—he managed to hide it for a while. When he realized he was dying, he put the rest of his money in Tia's star box, along with his map, and told us we'd have to go on to America without him. He said he'd given the captain instructions about where to send us when we got over here—only he didn't have faith in the captain, and was afraid something might go wrong. So he told us to pay careful attention while he explained what we'd have to do."

Tony stopped a moment while he tried to think. "I—I don't remember all he said. I couldn't possibly. But Tia does—only it got sort of blocked in her mind because of the things that happened. Anyway, it's coming back to both of us now. You know the rest of it—to the captain we were just another pair of refugees, and he didn't want to be bothered with us. So he called Mr. Deranian, who left us with Granny."

There was a long silence when Tony finished. At last Father O'Day got up and rebuilt the fire, and put the coffeepot on to boil.

He sat down, scowling, his battered face looking ferocious in the firelight. Suddenly he said:

"Do you remember where Uncle Bené wanted you to go? Was it to Stony Creek?"

"Yes, sir. And we were to see someone named Castaway."

"Castaway!"

"That's right. Tia remembered it last evening. But after all these years…"

"He may still be there. We'll look for him tomorrow. And it looks as if we can forget about Witch Mountain. Now, there's one thing that worries me. How much does that fellow Deranian know about you?"

"Not very much," Tony replied. "I heard him talking to that other man, Werner Karman, just before you called to us back at the Kozak place. Years ago, when he left us at Granny's, he had no idea those people abroad were looking for us. When he found it out, and they sent him to get us, it seems they didn't do too much explaining. They just warned him about us—told him he could expect almost anything…"

"Hmm." The priest rubbed a big hand over his jaw. "Obviously, the people who have been searching for you *knew* you would develop some very valuable abilities—even though you were both too young to show them at the time. They must have learned that from the other passengers in the lifeboat, the ones that weren't hurt too badly."

Tia nodded, and Father O'Day asked, "Do you know what happened to them?"

"They—they died," said Tony, repeating Tia's answer.

"And that left the two of you. Two small children who could be raised to do exactly as you were told. Two slaves with incredible abilities…" Father O'Day stood up. He looked as angry as Tony had ever seen him. "Why, Tony, your power of vision alone would be priceless to them! If they suspect you have that—"

"They know it," said Tony, with a glance at Tia. "She says Uncle Bené told us they'd found out that most of our family could vision distant places and see what was happening. I'm not good at it yet—"

"That makes no difference," the big man interrupted. "They know it, and they'll pay anything to get you back. If Deranian fails, they'll send others."

"Oh, no!" Tony was shaken.

"I'm afraid they will," the priest said slowly. "That's the sort of people they are. And it certainly complicates things."

"What are we going to do?"

"I don't know yet—except to keep you both hidden. A lot will depend on what we find at Stony Creek."

Tony looked unhappily at the fire. So much depended upon an unknown person named Castaway. Had they remembered him ten years too late?

Suddenly he thought of the witches again.

"I—I keep wondering about Witch Mountain," he said. "Why couldn't it have something to do with us?"

The priest shook his head. "How could it? As I told those men at the bridge, I've heard of the place—it was Augie Kozak who mentioned it to me. The only thing is, how could there be any possible connection between a group of so-called witches arriving at Witch Mountain—and you and Tia and some others being washed up on a communist coast after a shipwreck? Of course, both incidents seem to have happened at about the same time. But—"

Father O'Day stopped and stared at Tia. "What's the matter, my dear? *Is* there a connection?"

Tia did not answer. She was looking blankly into the fire. Tears glistened on her cheeks.

"Tia!" said Tony. "What's wrong?"

It was long seconds before she was able to answer. Finally she turned to him and told him.

Tony blinked at her. "It—it's all come back to her," he told the priest. "She says there *is* a connection between the witches and the rest of us who were wrecked. All of us came from the same place."

"Where in the world was that?"

"She—she says the place no longer exists."

"Eh? How do you mean?"

Tony swallowed. "It—it's one of the things Uncle Bené told us we must never forget. Tia remembers, and I've been remembering parts of it...You see, our old home was destroyed. We all managed to get away, for there were only a few of us left. Only, our ship burned before we got here, and we had to come the rest of the way in lifeboats. We were headed for Witch Mountain."

"You were headed for Witch Mountain—in *lifeboats?*"

"Yes, sir. But the lifeboat we were in ran out of fuel, somewhere in middle Europe. Tia says our parents were on board, and our father was pilot. If we hadn't been shot at, we could have landed safely. Instead we crashed."

Father O'Day gave a slight shake of his head as if he had not heard correctly. "What are you trying to tell me, Tony?"

Tony took a deep breath. What Tia had helped him to remember had been something of a shock, although he had guessed part of it.

"I—I'm trying to explain, sir, why my people called themselves the Castaways. Because that's what we are." He picked up Tia's star box and pointed to the design on it. "That's the emblem for our former home. We—we came from a planet that had two suns. A double star, really."

Father O'Day opened his mouth to speak, but could not. Finally he crossed himself, and sat down very slowly.

STONY CREEK

Tony glanced through the break in the foliage at the narrow strip of sky. It had paled slightly. Dawn could not be far away.

"Heaven preserve us!" the priest murmured finally. "I should have been able to guess something about you two, but I missed it entirely. My thinking has been so earthbound…There's just one thing—" He looked off into the night, his battered face puckered with bewilderment. "I don't understand about Witch Mountain. Why were the lifeboats going there? On all this planet, what was there about that particular spot that could have attracted your people?"

"Because we were mountain people, and it was a spot we'd chosen years ago," Tony explained. He listened to Tia a minute, and said, "Do you remember what the man told you at the bridge—that the first witches came to Witch Mountain in his grandfather's day? Well, I don't know how long ago that was, but it was when some of our people first came here."

"You mean on a sort of scouting trip?"

"Yes, sir. Somebody had to pick out a safe place to live, and go back and tell the others what to expect. They ran into all sorts of problems."

"I can see some of them. I imagine language…"

"Oh, they ran into a bigger worry than language. Tia says the scouts were amazed at the beauty of the planet, and shocked at the way people here were treating it. The only thing that mattered to them was money. It was their idea of wealth. Everything was based on producing it, and it was much more important than actually living and doing."

"Eh?" Father O'Day stared at him. "Living and doing? But, Tony, one has to have money merely to live and do."

"Sure, in *this* crazy place. But my people didn't know it when they first came here. And the people that were already here were not the kind that would go out of their way to help queer-looking strangers who couldn't talk English. Instead of helping you, they were more likely to shoot at you for trespassing."

"Ump. I see what you mean. If I'd come here scouting, and run into much of this world's meanness, I think I would have turned around and hunted for another planet—a better one."

"They wanted to, but they couldn't," Tony said. "There was no other place near enough that was habitable. So they picked a wild area, built a sort of station on the big mountain in the middle of it, and got busy learning the language and everything else they had to know. The big problem, of course, was land."

Father O'Day said grimly, "Land—the possession of it—has always been a problem. Half the wars on earth—"

"But we didn't know about that," Tony put in hastily.

"Didn't you own land where you came from?"

"Oh, no! *No* one owned it. It belonged to the planet. It was *part* of the planet, and everyone loved it and took care of it. Over here it belonged to *people*—and to be able to live on it safely and not be driven off, you had to *buy* it. Now do you see?"

"Oh!" said the priest, in dawning comprehension. "You really did have a problem." He scowled ferociously at the fire. "Imagine! A small group, advanced far beyond the idea of personal profit, coming to a greedy commercial world…forced to start a new life, knowing they couldn't afford to draw attention to themselves…needing a safe place to hide, so they could gradually blend in inconspicuously with the life around them…"

"So they had to buy land," Tony said quietly.

"Only, they had nothing they could use for money—or did they? What happened, Tony?"

"All I know," said Tony, "is that they stripped the scout ship of everything they figured they could get a few dollars for. Then they left two of the crew here to buy what they could, and hurried home to get the rest of us. That took years, of course—and all the time our old home was drifting closer to one of the suns…"

"Oh, good Lord! And you have no idea how the scouts you left here managed to make out?"

"No, sir. Everybody was studying English—until the ship burned—and we knew only that we were going to Witch Mountain. The name had got started before the scout ship left. When the scouts found out what it meant, they must have decided it would be a good name to keep."

Father O'Day chuckled. "Couldn't be better, since they wanted people to avoid the place. Now, about this Castaway at Stony Creek. Is he one of the scouts?"

"I—I don't know. Tia says Castaway is the name the whole group took, so I suppose everybody used it. We don't know who Uncle Bené wrote to, that time he got money for us to travel on after he escaped. It must be the same person we're supposed to see."

"Very likely. My guess, Tony, is that the group planned to use Stony Creek as an address in case of an emergency. If that's right, we ought to find a Post Office box there under the name of Castaway. Only, why did they use Stony Creek? That other place, Misty Valley, seems to be a lot closer to Witch Mountain."

A cold finger of doubt crept suddenly into Tony's mind. "I—I don't know," he faltered. "I was wondering the same thing."

Father O'Day went to the car and brought back a new road map and a flashlight. He spread the map on a blanket and turned the light on it. Tony watched his big finger move from town to town.

"The mountains are not given here," the priest muttered. "And it must be ten or twelve miles from Stony Creek to Misty Valley. Hmm. Well, there must be some very simple explanation for their choice of an address. We'll know in a few hours."

He put the map and flashlight back in the car, then moved the coffeepot to one side of the fire and placed a frying pan over the coals.

"Let's have an early breakfast and break camp," he said. "It will soon be daylight, and I've a feeling we've a very full day ahead of us."

The first golden shafts of sunlight were stealing through the trees when they were ready to leave.

Father O'Day stood frowning a moment at the muddy car. "I hate to give it a wash now," he said. "But for safety's sake, maybe we'd better. I'm sure Deranian knows that I'm down here. If no one has told him, he's certainly guessed it. And too many people will remember having seen a muddy car around…"

They filled the camp bucket from the stream and washed the car carefully, but left the license plate smudged so it could not be read too easily. Finally they were on their way, with Tony sitting on the floor again facing Tia and Winkie. The tarpaulin was stretched across the gear on the seat, ready to pull over them at a moment's notice.

"Before we get to Stony Creek," Father O'Day said presently, "we'd better face the fact that our hornless adversary is going to trace us there—if he isn't there already."

"But—how could he?"

"He can." The big man gave a rumbling growl that came from deep in his chest. "If I were superstitious, I'd say the fellow *has* got horns—I got a good look at him back at Augie's place and I could almost see the horns then. Anyway, if Uncle Bené told the captain of the Spanish ship where to send you, the destination might be remembered. If not, a fellow as clever as Deranian, horns or no horns—"

Suddenly Tony said, "Did I tell you he has another car full of men—four of them?"

"Ump! That's a detail you neglected to mention, and it doesn't do much for my peace of mind. I think I saw the car when I was crawling out of the orchard. Same make and color as the one he's driving. Both rentals, probably."

They swung into another road, and the priest said, "Just before I came down here, I phoned a friend of mine—a lawyer—and had him check on the legality of Deranian's claims to you. He *is* your legal guardian now, appointed by the court. If he gets his hands on you, the law's on his side. And I couldn't do a thing. In fact," he added with a low chuckle, "I could be arrested for kidnapping."

They reached a paved road finally, and later that morning rolled across the bridge into Stony Creek.

Father O'Day backed the car unobtrusively under some trees in sight of the main group of store buildings, and Tony raised his head cautiously above the seat to study the place.

It looked just as he had visualized it except that it was much more crowded now. His heart began to hammer as his eyes swept the parked cars and the groups of shoppers in front of the stores. This was the spot to which Uncle Bené, long years ago, had told them they must go to locate their people.

Would there be anyone here now named Castaway?

Father O'Day was scowling through the windshield. "Place is full of tourists," he muttered. "At least, we won't have to worry about witch hunters here. As for Deranian—"

"I don't believe he's here," said Tony. "Anyway, I don't see a car like the one he was using." Most of the cars in sight were either expensive machines or sport models.

"Well, you two keep under cover," the priest ordered, "and I'll go over to the Post Office and see what I can find out."

"Please," said Tony, "don't you think it would be better if I went with you? Tia can stay here and keep watch."

"What if Deranian, or some of his imps—"

"Tia can spot them. If I stay with her, we can't warn you without attracting attention. But if I'm with you, she can call to me and no one else can hear her."

"Oh. I'd overlooked that curious way the two of you have of communicating. O.K. Keep a sharp watch, Tia. Let's go, Tony!"

Tony slid from his hiding place and followed the big man across the street.

The Post Office occupied the narrow space between a grocery and a gift shop. Inside, a plump woman with gray hair appeared at the stamp window and said pleasantly, "Can I help you?"

"I most earnestly hope so," replied the priest. "We're trying to locate an old acquaintance by the name of Castaway. Could you tell us if any Castaways live around here?"

The woman's brow puckered, and Tony held his breath. "Castaway," she repeated. "Castaway." Slowly she shook her head. "No. If there had ever been anyone of that name around here, I would have remembered it."

Tony swallowed and tried to fight down a sick feeling.

Father O'Day said, "Have you been here long?"

"Nearly six years," she told him.

"Well, this goes back at least ten years, so he may have moved away before you came. There's a possibility he lived in Misty Valley. Does it have a Post Office?"

She shook her head. "All their mail is addressed to here, and delivered by rural carrier. It's not even on a bus route."

"Oh." The priest's eyebrows went up slightly and he glanced at Tony.

Tony thought, so *that's* why we were told to come here. Aloud he said, "Maybe, if we went over to Misty Valley…"

The woman said, "Just a moment. Maybe Grover knows." She turned and called, "Grover, didn't you have the mail route to Misty Valley before I came here?"

From somewhere behind a partition a muffled voice replied, "Shore did, ma'am. An' was I ever glad to give it up! That gap road in the winter was a pure fright."

"Grover, do you remember anyone on your route named Castaway?"

Tony pressed his clenched hands together. His knuckles began to whiten.

The unseen Grover drawled, "Castaway. Yep, there was a feller named that. Foreign, he was. Used to work at the old Lodge over there an' pick up their mail. That's how I happened to know 'im."

"Where is he now?" Father O'Day asked slowly.

"Gone to join his family. Had a big family, he told me once, but they was all sickly. Couldn't take the climate over here, an' they all died off. When I knowed Castaway, he was the only one left. Then I gave up my mail route, an' the Cooperative bought the Lodge. I hear he died a couple years later."

Tony's mouth began to tremble and he turned his face away to hide his tears. It was as if, suddenly, the world had come to an end.

He felt the comforting touch of Father O'Day's big hand on his shoulder, and heard him say, "What's this Cooperative you mentioned?"

"Misty Valley Cooperative, they call it. Just a bunch of city folks who wanted to get back to the country. Lot of 'em's dumb, so it's easy to see why they wanted to get away together. They bought up everything over there, I hear, so I reckon they ain't hurting none for money."

"Then all the Castaways are gone. But tell me this: do you know if there are any foreigners left over there who looked a little like the man you knew, or talked like him?"

"Nope," said the unseen Grover. "They're all plain Americans like you an' me, even them as can't talk."

"Thank you," the priest said, and silently guided Tony back to the car.

Tony could hardly bear to look at Tia as he told her what they had learned.

For a while afterward they sat in a brooding silence. Finally Father O'Day muttered, "Since we've come this far, I feel we ought to go on over to Misty Valley…"

"We—we can't go yet," said Tony. "Winkie hopped out of the car while we were gone. He hasn't come back."

The big man sighed. "Considering the kind of cat he is, I don't know whether that's a good sign or a bad one. Tia, how many were in that other lifeboat?"

"She says fifty," Tony replied. "Ours was much smaller. It held only ten."

"But *fifty!*" the priest exclaimed. He shook his head. "I should have realized what it was like for them, coming to a strange new world, with strange new ills that turned out to be deadly…Still, it does seem that a few…"

Tony said, "Tia and I have *never* been sick. Not once."

Something began to trickle through the back of his mind. He glanced at Tia, and saw that a curious look had come over her face.

Suddenly Tia whispered, "I've remembered something! *I'm* not the odd one, just because I *can't* talk. It's *you* who are odd—because you *can!*"

"Huh?" He gaped at her incredulously. The trickle in the back of his mind took form as he realized what she had said. His people had had no difficulty learning English. The hard part had been to *speak* it so those who spoke it naturally could *hear* it. Only a few of his people had been able to do that, and he was one of them.

All at once he said, "Tia, that map of Uncle Bené's—let's see it!"

She had already taken the folder from the star box and was opening it across her knees. Father O'Day twisted about in his seat and scowled at the map.

"Hey, what's come over you two?" the big man asked.

"Our people can't be dead," Tony said quickly, with rising excitement. "We—we think they've sort of covered up their tracks. Guess they had to. After Uncle Bené wrote to them, and they found out how we'd been treated, and what the world was like…"

"Eh? How d'you mean, Tony?"

"Well, if anybody managed to track them down, and even guessed at all the secrets they must know, like how to fly in space and all, think of the danger they'd be in."

"Oh, good Lord!"

Tony's finger touched the smudged words *Kiált Cast*, that Uncle Bené had written at the edge of the folder.

"Cast has to mean Castaway," he said. "What's the other word, Tia?"

The priest said, "I'm almost certain it's Hungarian—but why would he write in that language if he'd been studying English?"

Tia explained, and Tony said, "Our ship burned before we'd learned very much English. After we were captured we picked up a little of that European language. It must have been Hungarian. Anyway, when we didn't know the word for something in one language, we'd substitute a word from the other." He stopped abruptly and looked at Tia, and added, "*Kiált*—does it mean *telephone?*"

"He didn't know the word for telephone in either language, but what he wrote means *call* in English—so it's just as good."

"Of course! *Call Castaway.*" It was so simple and obvious that Tony wondered why he hadn't thought of it sooner. Immediately he began searching the street for a public telephone sign. He did not expect a place so small to have a booth, but he saw one beyond the gift shop in front of a parking area. On the instant he was sliding out of the car.

"Tony!" said Father O'Day. "What—"

"I'm going to make a phone call."

"But, Tony—"

"It's an idea—please pray we're right. Tia, explain it to him…" He turned and ran swiftly for the distant telephone booth.

Inside, he stood a few moments by the open door, trying to calm his excited breathing. Then he fished coins from his pocket and searched hastily through the book for the number he wanted. His heart started to pound furiously when he dialed.

The call went through quickly. In fact, the other receiver was lifted from the hook almost on the instant of the ring, as if someone had been waiting for it. But the man's voice that spoke into his ear was calm and unhurried.

"Misty Valley Cooperative."

Tony swallowed, and the receiver trembled in his hand as he groped for words. "I—I'm trying to find someone named Castaway," he blurted.

"Castaway?" the voice repeated in his ear. "I'll have to check on that. Who is calling, please?"

There was not the slightest indication that the speaker had ever heard the name before. His hopes went crashing again, but he managed to reply, "I—I'm Tony Castaway."

At that moment, abruptly, he heard Tia's silent cry of warning: "Tony—watch out! Mr. Deranian's car has just crossed the bridge—it'll pass right by you!"

WITCH MOUNTAIN

The shock of Tia's warning almost caused Tony to drop the receiver. He turned slightly, and out of the corner of his eye was able to glimpse a white sedan approaching slowly. Werner Karman was driving; Lucas Deranian sat beside him, his dark head thrust out of the window as he studied the cars in the parking lot. Behind the sedan came another very much like it that was filled with men.

Tony raised his right hand to the side of his head and hunched over the telephone book. The receiver in his left hand was vibrating strangely, but he hardly noticed it. All his attention was on the passing cars, which were creeping by hardly ten feet from the booth. It seemed impossible that six searchers could pass so close without one noticing him and investigating.

But they passed, and apparently no one looked at him twice. Then it came to him that only Mr. Deranian knew him by sight, and that his searchers would hardly expect to find him alone here on the street. More likely they were trying to locate Father O'Day's car. A muddy car, he hoped.

Suddenly he chilled as he saw that Mr. Deranian's sedan was swinging into the parking lot in front of him. At the same time he became aware of the vibration in the receiver, and he raised it to his ear.

"Toní! Toní!" a voice was saying urgently. "What has happened? Hurry—speak!"

For an incredulous moment Tony was incapable of replying. He had never heard Tia's voice on the telephone, for the simple reason that Granny had been too poor to have one installed. Because of that, he had not known that a telephone could transmit the sounds that were coming through the receiver now. High, rapid sounds that were beyond the range of earthly ears. It might have been Uncle Bené speaking to him—but it was the same person who had answered at first.

"I—I didn't know!" he managed to say. "I was afraid I'd made a mistake—the way you sounded when I asked you about the Castaways. I—"

"I had to make sure who was calling. Thank the blessed stars you've found us! We've been searching for you and Tia for years—as soon as we heard what happened at Fairview we started patrolling the roads, trying to locate you. We have seven cars on the road, and I'm in contact with all of them. Are you in Stony Creek now?"

"Yes, sir. I—I'm in the phone booth in front of the parking lot. But I'm afraid I'm sort of trapped here. I mean, the men who've been after us—there are six of them in two cars—have just driven past, and one car has turned into the parking lot."

"Were you noticed at all?"

"I'm sure I wasn't—but I'll be spotted for sure if I try to leave here." Tony glanced quickly around the back of the booth, and said, "Mr. Deranian—he's the only one who knows us by sight—is parked not fifty feet from me. He's sitting in the car watching the street. As long as he's there I can't possibly…"

"We'll get you away safely, never fear! Just hold on while I call the cars."

For a moment it seemed almost too good to be true. Tony peered down the street and saw that the second sedan had gone past Father O'Day's carefully washed car, apparently without noticing it, and was now vanishing around a curve. Then he risked another glance at Lucas Deranian, and a sudden coldness went through him.

More than once in the past few days he'd wished that Tia and he, among their other abilities, knew how to make themselves invisible. Now he realized it would take more than that to discourage Mr. Deranian—or the implacable people who were paying him.

If Tia and he escaped, with the help of the Cooperative, it wouldn't be long before the Cooperative came under suspicion. Then its secret, its precious and incredible secret that the surviving members of his race had worked so hard to hide, would be discovered.

Tony's face became grim. He'd seen too much of the world not to know what would happen. His people would be robbed, hounded, persecuted, and placed in constant danger for the rest of their lives.

"I won't do that to them," he muttered.

"Toní," the voice in the receiver said quickly, "one of us is driving over the Stony Creek bridge, and another—"

"Please," he interrupted, "tell 'em to stay away from me! I—I just realized what will happen. It'll be exactly as if I'd led that bunch straight to you. They'll find out everything. I—I don't know what to do about Tia—maybe you can figure out something—but as for me—"

"Toní!" the voice ordered. "Listen to me! You and Tia mean entirely too much to us even to dream of such a thing. Do exactly as we tell you, and *no* one will be in any danger. Understand?"

"But how—"

"There isn't time to tell you. There is too much to be arranged. First, where is Tia?"

"She's down the street, hiding in Father O'Day's car." He described it hurriedly and gave its location.

"Good! This may simplify matters. Give me a quick review of Father O'Day. Just what is he, and why is he concerned in this? How much does he know about you? Can he be trusted absolutely?"

"He's the only person who would believe the truth about us, and he's been helping us since we ran away from that juvenile home we were in. He knows everything about us—and there's nobody living I'd trust more. He—"

"That's good enough," the voice interrupted. "If you feel that way about him, we'll accept him without question. Now, you said that two cars were after you, and that the one with the man who knows you is in the parking lot. Where is the other one?"

"It went on through town—I can't see it. I'm sure the men in it were looking for Father O'Day's car—only they didn't recognize it because we washed all the mud off, and it looks so different—"

"Toní, call to Tia and have her tell Father O'Day we've worked out a plan, and to start driving toward you to pick you up. Quick, before the other car comes back!"

Keeping his face shielded with the telephone book, Tony turned to the open door, called and got Tia's attention, and hurriedly repeated the instructions.

The voice in the receiver said, "O.K., we're ready to move. I'm turning you over to Rael—he's been listening to this on his radio, and he's just stopped beside you."

Startled, Tony's eyes jerked to the green truck that had pulled up at the curb with the motor running. It was a sporty new truck, and the man driving it had the look of a prosperous young farmer.

Without looking at him, the man said in a silent rush, "Greetings, Toní! I'm Rael—though locally I'm listed as plain Ralph Jones. You've no idea how excited everyone is about you and Tia!" His hand flicked swiftly toward the parking lot. "Are those our sharpies in the white car?"

"Yes."

"We'll give them something to remember! I'm going to swing directly in front of them and block their view—that will give you a chance to get out of the phone booth without being noticed. We don't want them to guess you've been using the phone...Is that Father O'Day's car coming?"

"That's it."

"Then let's go! Get out of the booth as soon as I swing, and run up the street toward him."

Something about this maneuver worried Tony, but before he could ask questions Rael had gunned the truck motor and was turning into the parking lot. When the cab of the truck had shut off his view of Mr. Deranian's car, he dashed from the booth and began running up the street. But after a few paces he stopped abruptly. Ahead of him Father O'Day was slowing.

A small black cat had appeared out of nowhere, and had chosen this moment to cross the street. He was in no hurry, and he stepped along daintily, pausing every foot or two to look about and twitch his whiskers. It was Winkie.

Rael called silently, "Tony! What's the matter—are you afraid of a black cat?"

"No—that's Tia's cat! I—"

"Tia's? Then run and pick it up! Hurry!"

"But if I go any farther those men will see me!"

"Good! We *want* them to see you—now that you are away from the phone booth. They've got to recognize you and follow you. Understand?"

"Oh!"

Tony ran forward and snatched up Winkie. As he did so, the green truck backed and turned again, exposing him to the men in the white car. Out of the corner of his eye he saw Lucas Deranian stare at him, and suddenly speak urgently to the other man.

In the next breath, with Winkie safely in his hands, he was scrambling into the front of Father O'Day's car. As he slammed the door he heard Rael's silent order: "Straight ahead—cross the bridge the way you came into town, but take the left fork. I'll be right behind you."

Father O'Day said worriedly, "What's happening, Tony? I'm completely confused. Deranian has spotted us—"

"It's all right," he said. "He's supposed to follow us. It's part of the plan—whatever it is." He repeated Rael's directions, and glanced back as they crossed the bridge. Rael had cut in front of Mr. Deranian and was now directly behind them. Behind Rael came the white car. Tony glimpsed the second white car farther back, returning and hastening suddenly to catch up with them.

He thrust his head out of the window and warned Rael about the second car. Rael laughed and called back, "That's fine! We want them all in on this."

"What are you going to do?"

"We're trying to arrange things so they'll never look for you again."

"But if they get around you they can overtake us easy—"

"On a road like this, I doubt if they'll attempt it. Anyway, they couldn't pass me if they tried. Haven't you learned how to control another car from a distance?"

"I—I didn't realize it could be done!"

"Not all of us can—but after what you did in Fairview I'm sure you could manage it. Toní, when we reach the gap, I'm going to stop both cars. Then you must get out and run for it."

They were past the fork, and were beginning to climb on a winding road up a forested mountainside. Tia had thrown back the tarpaulin and was sitting up clinging to Winkie as she listened to Rael.

Tony called, "I don't understand! Where are we going, and where are we supposed to run after we get there?"

"You'll see," Rael told him. "There'll be someone to direct you. Do exactly as you are told. This is Black Gap Road—it takes you on over the mountains to Misty Valley. But you're not going past the gap…"

The road wound tortuously, climbing higher and higher. The three cars behind them dropped farther back. Father O'Day shifted gears; the grade increased as they crept above the trees and the old motor began to labor. Tony got out his harmonica in the hope that he could help it along but it was not necessary for all at once they were over the hump.

The forest was below them and they were rolling across what seemed to be a broad high meadow studded with boulders. It gave Tony the feeling of being on top of the world. Was this the gap?

It was, for suddenly the car stopped without warning, and he heard Rael's silent order. "Get out and run! Follow the path on your right!" Then the green truck swung past them, and dipped downward on the slope beyond the meadow.

They had already spoken their good-byes. Tia gave Father O'Day a final hug and tumbled out behind Tony clutching the star box in one hand and Winkie in the other. In their excitement and uncertainty the bags they had brought so far were forgotten, though it hardly mattered now.

Winding upward over the meadow was a vague path that led to an expanse of rock at the highest point. For an instant Tony hesitated seeing only the empty path leading to nowhere. To his right, a hundred yards down the road, he glimpsed the two white cars, stalled, and his sharp ears brought him the anger of the impatient drivers. When the men caught sight of him on the path, they began piling out to give chase.

At this moment of sudden doubt, Tony heard the silent instructions he had been listening for. He could not see the hidden speaker, but the voice was reassuring and he raced confidently up the path with Tia.

They reached the expanse of rock and scrambled to the top of it. Here all the world seemed spread before them—a tumbled world of mountains, half veiled in mist.

Far ahead, above one mountain darker than the others, something moved in the mist. It took silvery form, gleamed briefly as the sun touched it, and shot toward them with a speed and silence that brought an involuntary gasp from Tony. The thing coming to meet them looked almost like a flying saucer. With a shock of remembrance, he realized that was exactly what it was.

Down on the road, Father O'Day also gasped and made the sign of the cross. Though he knew he was seeing the second lifeboat, he had not expected it to look like this. The six panting men hurrying up the road to the path suddenly stopped and gaped in disbelief. From their angle of vision the approaching thing seemed to be swooping down from the skies. They saw it grow huge as it came close, to hover for a moment over the expanse of rock where the two small figures had climbed. When it moved and shot skyward, the figures were gone.

For a long minute afterward the six pursuers and the priest stood gazing upward in awed silence. Without a sound the thing had shot up, up, up, almost with the speed of light it seemed, to vanish in the remoteness of space.

Father O'Day was fingering his rosary, trying to compose his mind for a prayer, when he was interrupted by Lucas Deranian.

Deranian's face was grim. Through tight lips he bit out, "What was *that* thing?"

"You saw it," the big man told him. "It was nothing from this world. They finally remembered how to contact it."

"You're a liar! I don't swallow that sort of tale. It's all some devilish trick of yours—"

Father O'Day stiffened. "Don't ever confuse your master with mine!" he thundered. "Do you think the Lord on high is so frail that *this* little planet, with its greedy little people, is *all* that he can do? Bah!" Abruptly his great hand swept out, seized Deranian by the coat collar, shook him, and hurled him into the midst of the other men. "Get out of my sight! Go tell the rest of your kind there are marvels in Creation far beyond their narrow dreaming."

There were ugly mutterings, and for a moment it looked to Father O'Day as if he might have trouble on his hands. He smiled in sudden anticipation and took a step forward. There were six of them, but the Lord had given him a mighty body, and there was no better spot than a mountaintop for taking on the minions of the devil.

He was almost disappointed when they retreated to their cars. The motors started easily now, and he watched in considerable satisfaction while they turned the cars around at the edge of the meadow, and drove back the way they had come.

After a long while he followed them. He would rather have gone in the opposite direction, but he wanted his first view of Witch Mountain to be in the dusk, when he could catch the homey glow of lights through the mist, and hear again the magic of music that would never be forgotten. After all that had happened, he knew it would be much wiser to wait a while before he joined the children on Witch Mountain.

ABOUT THE AUTHOR

Alexander Key started his career as an artist, studying at the Art Institute of Chicago. He then pursued a successful career as an illustrator of children's books, which soon led him to write his own. Key is the author of many popular science fiction stories for children including *The Forgotten Door*, *The Golden Enemy*, and *The Incredible Tide*.